Blue Water Red Blood

D L Havlin

Double Edge Press

Scenery Hill, Pennsylvania

Double Edge Press

ISBN 978-1-938002-09-0

Dedication

To: Lillian Bradley

Librarian extraordinaire,
at
The Lee County Library's
Pine Island Branch

Other Titles by D L Havlin:

The Cross on Cotton Creek

A Place No One Should Go

The Hangin' Oak

September on Echo Creek

Story Time-R

Blue Water Red Blood

D L Havlin

Acknowledgements

I used to read acknowledgements with little or no appreciation and with less feeling for the author and those cited. No more! After my writing journey of the last 17 years, I truly know the value of those who vitally contribute to the success of any author on their quest to produce a worthwhile work.

My first major debt is to Babs Brown and Robert Fulton, Ph.D., my patient, skillful, editors, and to authors Bev Browning and Mary Ann Evans, both mentors whose efforts have immeasurably improved my craft.

I owe a second special thanks to my publisher, Double Edge Press and to its editor-in-chief, Rebecca Melvin. Without her belief in my work and writing skills, there'd be no book titled "Blue Water Red Blood."

The third special debt is to my 'beta' readers, past and present, who took the time to critique my work. Present readers Chet Collins, Tonya Player, Paul Owen, Judy Galinski, Sandra Pirman, Jeanne Miller, Carol Robb, Gayle Marie Hackbarth-Harting, Todd Sharp, Pat Cole and Andrew Schickowski combine their criticism with suggestions and encouragement. Their backgrounds, including high school principle, teacher, editor, book store owners and managers, lit majors and seminary grad, (ages 28 to 64) help them provide invaluable feedback. Their comments such as "I hope you understand this for no one else will," "Provide alarm to wake reader when chapter 6 is complete," "Ya-da-da-da-da," and *"Bullus shitus,"* kept me on track; and "Written with heart and conviction," "I cried and I don't do that often," "Wonderful thoughts written in beautiful prose," "This is twelve on a scale of ten," fired my enthusiasm to write the next page, chapter, and book.

Finally, I reserve my largest, most heart-felt thank you for my loving wife, partner, do-everything assistant . . . Jeanelle. Without her support, encouragement, understanding and tolerance I would have abandoned writing long ago.

Foreword

Blue Water, Red Blood is the story of fantastic coincidence and intersection of fates that marked the LVT, or "Alligator's," development. This is the amphibious tractor our brave Marines rode into battle when they fought the bloody Pacific island conflicts during World War II. More properly, it's a testament to the exceptional men that "made it happen." While many of the events and characters portrayed in this book are historically accurate enough to teach a class from, I ask the reader to keep in mind this is a novel.

When writing historical fiction, I'm always concerned about blurring the line between fact and fabrication. Since *Blue Water, Red Blood* deals with so many historical events and characters, and fewer than normal concocted ones, this concern is heightened. Here is a guideline for you to remember when reading this book. Chapters 1, 16, and 24 are non-historical, totally fictional in nature, and in them, some pains have been taken to separate reality from fiction. For example, Ben Bennett is cast as a member of the 2nd Marine Battalion, company "J." However, company J didn't exist as a Marine designation. These three chapters are plates used to serve the "meat" contained in the remainder of the novel.

All other chapters are based on historical happenings. While historically accurate in regard to the events, in most instances the situations portrayed and the interchanges between characters, historical and otherwise, are fictional. They're provided to the reader for their interpretive value; to set scope and the point of view of the main characters involved. Examples are the event commonly known as the Rape of Nanking portrayed in Chapter 11 and the party conversation at which Roebling's "Alligator" rescue amphibian was referred to the Marines in Chapter 12. They present facts that transpired during these events, but neither the Nanking episode nor the exact party dialogue actually occurred. Each was written to illustrate the incident and was a calculated guess on my part.

You'll bump into historical giants, men that shaped the life and death struggle that was World War II. Donald Roebling, Holland Smith, and Andrew Higgins are the preeminent figures used to tell this story of patriotism and achievement. The personal traits of the real-life characters are based on the best information I could glean from the histories, biographies and autobiographies I researched. Their conversations are fabrications with a few major exceptions—Admiral King's confrontations with Holland Smith during their first time working together, Nimitz's informing Smith of his promotion as Commander of Marine invasion forces in the Pacific, and Smith's statement "No tractors, no invasion," when giving an ultimatum to Kelly Turner regarding the Tarawa landings.

As mentioned, most of the characters appearing in *Blue Water, Red Blood* were living human beings. Among those you'll get a "hand shake" from are: John "Black Jack" Pershing, Admiral Chester Nimitz, Admiral Kelly "Terrible" Turner, Admiral Ernst J. King, President Franklin Roosevelt, General John Russell, John Roebling, and Ada Smith—"Howling Mad's" wife and rudder. There are more mentioned. Many of the people associated with the military or Roebling's machine development effort actually played their historical part. The Marines mentioned in chapter 21 are all fictional as are all Bennett family members.

One person doing a preliminary read on *Blue Water, Red Blood* was convinced I'd uncovered new information or had witness input as background for the conversations written in the novel. I want to be clear that there are *no* "previously undiscovered papers" or "witnesses" to serve as foundations for dialogues in the book. I believe misleading anyone by turning fiction into fact is an authorship sin.

When I graduated from college in the mid-sixties, I was fortunate to be employed by FMC Corporation in Lakeland, FL, the company and location that produced the LVT. This amphibious tractor, so crucial to our victory in the Pacific during World War II, was the ancestor of the M-113 personnel carrier, the Bradley fighting vehicle, and others that still serve in our military today, and were also manufactured by FMC. During my early years with the company, many of those who were involved in the tractor's production were still working there. I heard many stories about the manufacture of the unit and stories about Don Roebling, one of this novel's principle characters. He was as eccentric as portrayed in this book, and if just some of the oral history passed along by my old cohorts is true, much more so.

These stories combine with tales told by a relative who fought in the Pacific and who was more passionate about the Marine Corps than his wife or life itself. He fought in horrendous places. However, Tarawa wasn't one of them. His stories about Peleliu and other horrible battles, his dedication to his brothers-in-arms, and his unquenchable hate for his past enemies fascinated the young me. He landed in the tractors invented by Roebling. Among the Marine Corps heroes and leaders he deified was Holland Smith. As it would happen, the products of Smith and Roebling's efforts, if not their paths, are intertwined.

The story related in this book is not only an interesting tale of how unrelated incidents can converge to form history, but also a look at how the experiences of the historical characters shaped their destiny and the lives of many others. Their stories also provide some important life lessons in the telling.

While researching *Blue Water, Red Blood* I was fascinated to find two common personal attributes were abundantly possessed by the story's three very different historic heroes, Roebling, Smith, and Higgins. Because each was endowed with these character enrichments, they achieved their goals. Identifying these traits is a challenge I'd like you to accept as you read this book. Answer the question, "Do I possess those traits as part of my makeup?" for your own introspection.

Since fiction is what I do, my prime directive is to entertain. But, I also strongly believe *readers are thinkers*. When I write, I strive to satisfy this reader need as a clear second objective. In the realm of historical fiction, the opportunity exists to provide copious quantities of cuisine for hungry minds. It's one of the reasons I love the genre. I hope this novel, may, in some way, feed yours.

DL Havlin

Table of Contents

Table of Contents (continued)

Table of Contents (continued)

Table of Contents (continued)

1

Return to Tarawa
2009, Ben Bennett
Kiribati, the Island of Betio, Tarawa atoll

They were gone and that was wrong. His memory protested. No orange flame-shrouded landing craft lay in the blue Pacific water, billowing black smoke into the tropical sky. No shell and bomb craters disturbed the sand on which he stood. No discarded combat equipment or first aid leavings littered the ground. No topless palm trees and burning buildings. No smell of cordite. No stench from the dead. No Marines huddled fearfully, clutching their weapons, cursing, praying, behind a seawall that had since disappeared. No bloated, dust covered Jap bodies . . . and . . . no brother Marines, who gave their all, lay on the beach or floated in the waters that lapped the shore. Only the white sand and blue water remained as recorded in his mind. His back rebelled as he reached down and scooped up a handful of white-gray granules and let them sift through his worn fingers. Yes, he was really back. He closed his eyes.

The old man took a deep breath as his emotions seethed. Closing his eyes made *that* other beach reappear: the one covered with those fractured palm trees, pock marks from bombs and naval shelling, fragments of buildings, burning military vehicles and the flotsam of battle.

The din of combat filled his mental ear: the thud of bursting mortar shells, the zing of bullets, the staccato chatter of machine gun fire, the crack of rifles . . . the screams of the wounded, the dying. And, though he tried to shut them out, invariably they came, those sights of twisted, grotesque, deteriorating corpses, both Marine and Japanese. Ben opened his eyes before dead friends entered his vision and tears betrayed him.

He gazed down the beach in one direction, then in the other, looking for any of the sights living vividly in his memories that time hadn't wiped away. Very few remained to remind him of the momentous, horrible event which was burned into his consciousness sixty-plus years before. The landmarks and features he searched for were gone—with the exception of a few preserved for their historical importance and their value as tourist attractions and those which nature decreed were permanent. Benjamin Bernard Bennett, SN# X54670, USMC, found it hard to believe neat modern structures occupied the sacred sand. His mind had preserved the island's portrait so perfectly from his last glimpses of the battleground those many years before; could this really be the same place? That was a landscape of terror, of fear, of unspeakable sights . . . of death. This beach was an idyllic paradise.

Ben never thought he'd live to see this place again. He'd talked to his family about visiting without serious intent. His service in the Second World War was the event that most shaped his life and how he looked at it, and, naturally, it was something about which he occasionally spoke. His family honored him and therefore his desire; that was why they were on the island beneath his feet. But when Ben talked to his friends and family about life in the Marines, it was about places he'd been stationed, or escapades on leave, or buddies—not bodies, not the details of what happened at this place. He shook his head and his body shuddered slightly.

"You okay, Dad?" his son, Andy, asked. It was Andy who planned the surprise trip. He stood a few steps behind Ben and Andy was accompanied by his wife and boy, Ben's grandson. Ben looked at them, then at his grandson's wife and his great-grand-children walking the beach two hundred yards away. They were bending over to pick up sea-shells where his fellow Marines bent over to avoid bullets and shells of another variety those many years ago.

"Yeah, I'm fine." He took a deep breath.

"I guess it looks completely different than it did then." Andy watched his father, not the beach or the other members of his family.

"Yes, it does, Andy." Like many combat veterans, Ben preferred to let the horrors he'd seen and the terrors he'd experienced in battle lie buried in his soul. But, they were part of him, and, like it or not, they occasionally exhumed themselves. Those unwanted memories restated their claim to immortality in his mind at such times. This was one. When he spoke of these stored nightmares, it was with moist eyes, through tight lips. Despite the horrible recollections and deep bitter feelings, Ben could not separate from the magnet that is the past. Tarawa was the horror dream which visited most frequently. It was his first and worst combat experience. He shook his head, "It's like this is . . . wrong. It shouldn't be this way. It's . . . it's . . . nice. I guess I never thought about what it would be like now. I knew it would be different than when we landed, I just never thought about . . . this."

"You recognize anything at all?"

"The island hasn't changed much, just what's on it. And, what's gone. That's completely different. The image has been so strong in my mind for so long—" The ghosts were close, his voice tightened; he stopped speaking. This tiny island had taken part of his soul during the four-day lifetime he spent there starting November 20, 1943. He knew his comrades had done their part. He was *sure* he'd done his, but for what? His unanswered question remained: was his sacrifice and the blood of his fellow Marines that spilled into the pure blue waters surrounding Betio worth the victory?

"Is this where you came ashore?" His grandson was eager to hear stories that Ben wished to keep to himself. The young man's curiosity was that of an individual who saw war as a movie, not as an event that friends die in or that smelled of decomposing bodies.

"I'm not sure," Ben said. He squinted and tried to orient himself. "Let me think."

"Take your time, Dad, it'll come to you, it's been a long time," Andrew said reassuringly.

Ben slowly examined the scene in front of him from right to left and said, "We're close." He stepped toward the lagoon where there was a small, but steep, slope that led to the beach and the coral reefs beyond. He mumbled more to himself than to anyone else, "This is where the old seawall was. I think this is Red 3. I came ashore on Red 2." He motioned toward a cove farther down the beach where languid waters peacefully lapped the shore. "I know that was Red 1," Ben said with increasing surety. He was oblivious of his family following behind. He pointed to his left, "The pier was there." His arm moved a little farther and he said confidently, "It was right over there."

"It's great that you did what you did here." Ben's grandson's flattery was sincere. Then he asked a question that he believed would return their conversation to the reason for their journey. "I know it's been sixty years, but can you tell us what it was like? What was going on inside of you?"

"I've spent sixty years trying to forget . . . *what it was like*. I never stopped reliving this place since the day I got off of it. Remembering is *too* easy. Talking about it, that's something different." Fire glowed in the old man's eyes. "I don't like to talk about it because I don't like thinking—" Ben quit speaking in mid-sentence.

"Sorry, Gramps," Mark, look crushed and guilty.

His reaction made Ben feel guilt of his own. "Ahhh, I shouldn't have said that. It's natural for you to be curious. Going into detail is difficult enough for me. Getting inside my thoughts? It's impossible to understand what goes on inside somebody like me unless you have a feel for what goes on in this kind of fighting."

"Grandpa, I've read so much about this battle, saw so many pictures and have seen a bunch of documentaries—well, I think I've got a good feel for it."

The old man sighed and shook his head. "I know you'll probably be offended by what I'm going to say. Try not to be. I know you want to make me feel good. I appreciate that. Do I think that what you've seen and heard allows you to know what happened here? Yes, probably. Do you have the same vision and feelings as the men that made the landing? Believe me, you don't. Can I describe them in a way you could connect? No. Not one of those books you read screams in pain or begs for its mother. None of the photographs smell of death so bad you have to constantly fight the urge to vomit. None of those documentaries shows your best friend being a man one second and a pile of hamburger the next. Corpses you see on those old films aren't men you've shared meals, trained and lived with. My words can't make you feel the indecision and fear you have each time you move. Those pieces of paper and tape are *things* that can tell you about events—my words won't do any better—but neither can instill the *emotions* that being there does. The horror and fear you had living it . . . the pride in surviving and triumphing in such terror . . . the guilt from asking the question, 'why did I live when so many didn't?' You can try, but you'll never get to that depth. What happened to me and each man that was here is personal and different. It's difficult to put into words something that's so private to you. And, honestly, even if I could, I wouldn't."

Mark looked upset but remained silent. His eyes' focus shifted to the Pacific.

"Mark, what your Grandpa is saying is that anyone who's not been in the kind of fighting like he experienced, or to some degree, what I did in Vietnam, can't understand," Andy said calmly. "You can't, because there's nothing in your life that *even approximates* what happens in fighting like what happened here."

"Gramps, I don't want to crawl inside your soul. Honest. I understand you don't want to share that. It would be wrong for me to intrude." Mark took a breath. "What about describing what you did, step by step? Not what you were thinking, just what happened."

The old man nodded. "You say you've read about the invasion so you know the Navy thought we'd be able to walk ashore carrying umbrellas instead of rifles because of all the shells they fired at the island. Well, they fired a lot and a lot missed. There were 5000 Japanese on Betio, the pre-landing bombardment killed quite a few, but most were left for us. You know all that. Well, what I thought was bad luck turned out to be good. I was assigned to land in the first wave hitting the beach. That's normally who take the worst casualties. It meant I had a lot better chance of getting killed, I thought. We were assigned the new LVT as our landing craft. They moved slower than the Higgins boats that later waves were assigned to land in. But they were tracked vehicles and could plow through barbwire and take you right up on the beach. The Higgins boats took about three feet of water to float in."

Ben pointed to waves breaking over the reef 600 yards off-shore. "We took some shelling before we got to the reef, but the Alligator, that was the name for the LVT, ground right over it. As soon as we got there, the Japs cut loose with everything they had. Mortars, artillery, machine guns, the works. The first wave took a lot of hits, but my LVT got us on the beach and delivered me and my platoon right up behind the seawall. We scrambled over the sides and had the palm logs that formed the wall for cover. My platoon lost men in the first few minutes, but we were able to clean out some of the emplacements in the seawall. That gave us a measure of protection."

Ben looked down the beach. "The second wave was in LVTs, too. Just like in my wave, some got hit by mortars or artillery and burned like a son-of-a-bitch. Most of them got in, dropped the men on the beach and took off. When the third wave came in, we found out how lucky we'd been to be in the LVTs. Only some of the men in that wave were in Alligators. The rest were in Higgins Boats. They couldn't make it over the reef because it was too shallow. Those guys got dumped out there. They had to wade ashore. The Japanese cut them to shreds. Machine gun fire was the worst. The largest number of men killed in any part of the battle was right out there. All the following waves were in Higgins Boats. The slaughter repeated each time a new wave was unloaded."

"Damn, how did any of them make it in?" Andy asked.

Ben shook his head. "Luck or God's protection. The Jap positions were dug into the ground and had narrow fields of fire. They'd originally been set up so they interlocked. If a man was lucky enough to be wading in through a corridor where the guns had been destroyed by the naval bombardment or at a spot where we that had already landed and killed the gunners, he had half a chance. There was a pier that stuck way out to the outer edge of the reef. A lot of the men that were close enough to that structure waded over to it and came in using it for cover. But in general, it was a massacre."

The old man became silent. The only sound was the sea-breeze rustling through the fronds of a near-by palm. His family let him gather his composure that had been slipping away. Ben realized they were patiently waiting for him to regroup. He carefully phrased his next words to protect his psyche from what he knew would come if he went into too great of detail. After taking two deep breathes, he said, "It was so hard, being crouched behind those logs . . . you could see men getting cut to ribbons. You got mad, but there was little you could do. We killed the gunners that had guns set in the seawall and a few right behind it, but going over those logs right then was sure death. Some really brave or really foolish men tried, not many survived. Of those who made it, a few were able to destroy some of the little yellow bastards before they got killed themselves. Later, we saw evidence of what some Marines did. Very few of the first guys over the wall survived the battle."

Ben pointed to the reef. "The LVT drivers saw what was happening. They started picking up wounded to take to the boats that were milling around out there. The drivers transferred the casualties to Higgins Boats to go back to the ships. Then they started ferrying in men that were on the reef. They met Marines coming in Higgins Boats, transferred them into the LVTs and brought them to the beach. I don't know how many trips they made, but without what they did, a larger number of men would have been killed. Those drivers were really brave. They brought in ammunition and all kinds of things we needed and wouldn't have survived without."

"Do you think some of those things that looked like rusting piles of metal we saw lying out in the water as we walked along the beach could be old LVTs?" Andy's wife asked.

"Yes, they could be. Those ugly hunks of iron sure looked beautiful on November 20, 1943. When I was huddled behind the seawall, trying to stay alive and do what I could to fight, one of the guys said, *"Hey 3B,"* that was my nickname, *"We need to get Chaplin Kelly to say a prayer for those LVTs and their drivers. They're all that's keeping us alive."* Bennett looked at his great-grandchildren playing at the waters edge then pointed to them. "I hope none of them have to go through it, but, the way things are today, they probably will."

"Damn, I hope it doesn't come to that." Andrew Bennett shook his head and looked disgusted. "You're probably right. With the way the world is today, it doesn't look good."

"I pray you're both wrong," Andy's wife said. "I don't know if I could stand to see the boys go off to war." Andy and Mark agreed by nodding their heads.

"Doesn't seem that we humans learn, does it?" Mark said.

"I guess not," Ben said. He stared at the water. "I wish we could. The problem is humans don't want to learn. If there's anybody in this world that hates war more than me, I'd like to be introduced to them. As much as I hate it, there are times you don't have a choice. There'll always be those who believe they have the right to impose their will on others. Leaders lead and the people follow. Hell, look at what's going on in the Middle East. It's what happened in Germany and Japan in the '30s all over again. They want to take what we have and we don't want to give it up. They have a set of ideals they believe in and how to achieve them. They're diametrically opposed to ours in many ways. The radical Muslims are as fanatical as the Nazis and Japanese militarists were. Potentially, there's a lot more Muslims who can be drawn into a future conflict, whether they want to be or not. The base of men Hitler and Tojo had to draw from was much smaller, so it's a lot more dangerous for us."

"We may not have a choice if the radicals have their way, unless we all want to become Muslims and live in the 14th Century. I'm guessing a lot of us will have to fight." Andy shook his head. "World War III . . . that will be one horrible affair. Nuclear bombs, chemical weapons, biological agents, plus things like gas and napalm from before make the carnage too terrible to contemplate. There is probably stuff we don't even know about. I hate to imagine what it would be like. Unfortunately, people who welcome death as a reward won't see it that way."

"Aren't most of those things, I mean the weapons, illegal to use anymore?" Ben's grandson asked.

"What's legal and what isn't doesn't mean much if your survival is in the balance. I saw it here in the Pacific. Neither the Japs or us worried about laws and rules." Ben's eyebrows lifted. "Both sides will do anything they can to win . . . to live."

Andrew nodded. "You're right, Dad. You don't think about the proper way to kill someone who wants to kill you. I saw that everyday in Vietnam."

"Warfare was a hell of a lot different in 1943 than it is today," Ben said. "There weren't any missiles—no airplanes that could fly to Japan, drop bombs and return to the US. When we landed here, 600 miles was about the longest range any of our planes could fly. The only way we could defeat the Japanese was to seize their islands for air bases that stretched across the Pacific so we could attack them. They killed us and we killed them just about any way possible."

"An amphibious assault is the most dangerous and costly type attack you can be engaged in. That's what it took to get those bases." Andrew looked at his son. "Look at that beach. There's no place to take cover. Think about having to jump out of a boat, wading through waist deep water and running up over that sand with hundreds of mortars, machine guns, and thousands of riflemen shooting at you. When you get there, you can't even see most of the enemy because they're in camouflaged holes, bunkers and pill boxes. It's frontal attack of the bloodiest variety."

"Damn, that's an 'Oh shit!' moment if I ever heard one," Mark said. He looked at the reef, the hundreds of yards of water between the barren expanse of sand at the waters edge and where he imagined the seawall was during the battle. "That's asking more from a human being than it seems possible to expect."

"Mark, you just have to hope that you have leaders that do what they can to protect you, even if they're asking you to risk your life." Ben looked the young man in the eye. "I had a good one. Chances are I wouldn't be here without him. I wouldn't have been in one of those LVTs I was telling you about without having the particular general that commanded the Marines, here in the central Pacific."

"What was his name, Gramps?"

"Holland Smith. There wasn't anybody any tougher. Maybe Patton was as tough, but a Marine has a hard time giving Army men much credit. His nick-name was, Howlin' Mad Smith, because he generally seemed to be that way. He had a tough job that had to be done. Smith knew he'd be sending a lot of us to our death. But he really cared for us and tried to protect his troops the best he could. I saw him a couple times. He was older than most of the field command generals. Smith was called the father of amphibious warfare. He developed a lot of the tactics. I know he fought with the Navy to get us a good landing craft. Old Howlin' Mad was responsible for getting the Higgins Boat and the Alligator adopted by the Marines for our use. I don't know a whole lot more about that, except the LVT was an outgrowth of a rescue vehicle developed by some guy name Roebling. Back a few years, I read an article or two about him and Higgins, the guy the boats are named after. Other than knowing both of them had to fight Washington to get their craft accepted, and that Roebling's grandfather built the Brooklyn Bridge, I don't know as much as I guess I should, considering that they helped save my life."

"Grandy Ben, look here! Isn't this a big one?" Fifty yards away one of Ben's great-grand-daughters stood knee deep in the Pacific holding a large seashell above her head. Her shouts were quickly followed by her mother's upset yelling, "Amber, you've got good shoes on! Get out of the water!" The woman waved at her husband, Mark, and added, "Please go down and get her and make her stay out of the water."

"I'll be right back after I try to complete mission impossible."

"Let's all go," Andy's wife suggested. They all started for the water's edge—except for Ben.

"I'd like to be alone for a little while. You all go down there. I'll join you in a few minutes." Ben watched them walk down the slope to the beach. After they glanced back a time or two, their focus shifted to the children frolicking at the shores edge.

Ben faced the lagoon, closed his eyes and took a deep breath of the salty sea breeze. He purposely allowed his mind to recreate an image of the men wading over the reef to the shore where he stood. Because there weren't enough LVTs for all the Marines, grievous wounds or death was the probability, not just possibility, for them. Those men moved unflinchingly onward, falling forward or back when struck by the wall of lead and steel streaking toward them. Some wounded men struggled on through the water; others, torn to shreds, screaming, cursing, bleeding, dying, fell into the red tinged blue. For a few seconds it was 1943 again. The terrible sights, sounds and smells rushed back. Ben opened his eyes to end the horror movie in his mind.

The Alligator and the men who struggled to provide it were what made it possible for him to have the memory. Though it was a horribly disturbing one, it was better than than being a corpse in some other man's nightmare. For this, he was truly thankful. Ben decided that he'd pay homage to those men in the only way he could; he'd learn about them when he returned home, feeling that gaining this knowledge would honor them in some small measure. So strange, he thought, that a vehicle designed to save lives in peacetime never did, but became one that saved so many in war. The LVT that delivered him 'safely' to the shores of Hell was originally conceived to rescue hurricane victims from another type of Hell, one made by nature, not man.

He stared at the lagoon and said to himself, "I'd loved to have met Roebling and Smith. Maybe Higgins. It seems wrong not to get a chance to talk to someone, to get to know them, to thank them for helping save your life. I would have liked to know what made them tick. What were the stories behind what they did? Where did it all start?" Ben's mind drifted backward, lost in thought, wondering about his saviors and what coincidences aligned to allow his feet to rest on the sands under him.

2

Learning About War
1918, Holland Smith
Pershing's Headquarters, France

"Not him either. He's too much of a politician." General John J. Pershing scowled at his aide. "I don't want to send somebody out there that will tell me what he thinks I want to hear. An after action report isn't worth the paper it's on if it doesn't tell the clear, unvarnished truth. And don't suggest some staff officer that doesn't have blood on his bars. The last thing I want is some asshole who's never been shot at and doesn't know what the hell goes on in battle telling me what went wrong. Who have we got that we can send out that will be honest, doesn't mind poking through the gore and carnage on that field and won't give a damn if he hurts his chances for his next promotion?" Pershing shoved a couple of file folders back across his desk at a deflated looking Colonel Charles E. Stanton.

The aide took a deep breath. "I'll have to take another look at who we have that will fit with the other officers going out there."

"Fit? Fit?! Fit!! I don't want an officer that can dance. I want one who isn't afraid to kill the damn musicians. Charlie, I want somebody with combat experience who will be critical, but honest. Dead honest. I don't care if he's an anti-social bastard. You mean we don't have anyone on the staff like that?" Pershing's eyes had fire in them.

"Are you willing to reassign a higher ranking officer?" Stanton asked.

"Who did you have in mind?"

"What about Colonel Patton. He certainly isn't bashful about expressing his opinion." Stanton knew of Pershing's knowledge of, and fondness for, the man.

Pershing didn't hesitate, "He's precisely what I'm looking for, but he's too valuable where he's at. He's the only officer we have that really understands how to use tanks and isn't afraid to get out and fight with the troops. Who else?"

"Critical." The aide thought and a faint smile formed on his lips. "Do you remember meeting with that young Marine officer from the 4th Brigade? He was the Adjutant with them. I know he's seen significant action here and in the Philippines. I think he had a citation for the fighting that he was in during the Dominican Republic thing. He's the first Marine ever to attend the Army General Staff College. The man is real sharp. Right now he's assigned as an assistant operation's officer in your staff. He's been a communications officer. He sounds like exactly what you're asking for."

"What's his name?"

"Holland Smith."

Pershing's head moved back and his eyes shone. "Oh, yes. I remember him for several reasons. He's like me, he's known as well by his nick-name as by his given name. That gives us something in common, doesn't it?"

"Black Jack and Howlin' Mad," Stanton smiled, "That's quite a pair."

"General Harbord recommended him highly. That means a lot. Jimmie Harbord's a real fighting man." The General leaned back in his chair. "Did you know Smith turned down an appointment to West Point?"

"No. To join the Marines and do the same thing? That doesn't make sense."

"Harbord told me about it. His parents wouldn't let him accept the appointment his congressman got for him. Seems they're still fighting the Civil War. They're from Russell County, Alabama, and still hate the government. He went to college, didn't like what he was doing and ended up in the Marines. Harbord also told me . . . he . . . *is* . . . tough."

"Well?" Stanton waited for Pershing's answer.

Pershing stared into space. After a delay of a long half-minute, he said, "No. He'd do a fine job, but half the people reading anything he wrote would ignore it because he's a Marine. There's a lot of Army officers who can't understand why there even is a Marine Corp, think the men in it are amateurs, and, bottom line, they're still part of the Navy, even though half the Naval personnel themselves don't have any use for Marines."

"How about you, General?"

"Marines are very good troops. I saw what they could do at Belleau Wood. But I don't have time to fight the Army brass about accepting a Marine's opinion of our battle efficiency any more than I do fighting with Wilson over allowing me to integrate Negro soldiers in our forces. Both would be time wasted. Who else can you think of?"

"What about Marshall? I know he's on the planning staff, but I think he'd do the job. Evaluating what you planned for others to do; should be enlightening."

"George Marshall will do an honest job. He's as good as we have. Let's use him, Charlie." Pershing looked at Stanton. "Howlin' Mad Smith was a good idea. Keep him in mind for some future assignment." Pershing cocked his head to the side and grinned. "Nick-names can change. Mine's better than what it was. Since I got my last star they don't call me Nigger Jack anymore. Maybe his will change as he goes up—and he will go up."

* * *

Coblenz, Germany, January, 1919

"I agree, Holland. It's stupid to keep throwing troops into frontal assaults when you know what the result is likely to be before you send them out of the trenches." Pete Ellis put his feet up on his desk. "It doesn't make any difference how far we had to go to flank those trenches. That's what we needed to do. And, I agree, it has nothing to do with you not wanting to fight. Anybody that knows you has no questions about your willingness to go into a battle. But, charging across those no-man's lands was suicide; a complete waste of fine troops."

"They needed to study what Lee did at Chancellorsville." Major Holland Smith pointed to markings on the paper lying in front of him. "Petain could have left a third of his army in the trenches and slid the rest to the right. Who cares if you get detected or have to go through some terrain that's not perfect for fighting. Anything's better than running across open fields into the German prepared positions and trenches. If we could have ever gotten them out of their holes, we could have whipped their asses without the casualties we took." He drew some arrows on the paper, then tapped the pencil point on the desk until it snapped off. "Pete, I'll never waste men's lives in a frontal assault like that. Maneuver and speed. That's the way to attack."

Ellis cocked his head to the side. "What if you don't have an option?"

"You can always find an option, Pete. I don't want to be the officer responsible for ordering a thousand men out of a trench, watch them made into a gory mess of severed arms, legs, and entrails and see half or less struggle back to where they've started without accomplishing a damn thing. Try a flanking movement, use small infiltration groups like the Japanese do, or hell, retreat far enough to draw your enemy forward and pinch off his advance. Attacking fixed lines and fortifications just gets men killed."

"If your superior says, 'attack here, in this way,' what are you going to do?"

Smith looked at his friend, hesitating as he thought about the question. "If it was an order to march my men into a meat grinder, with no chance of success, I'd try talking the command into an alternate plan I'd provide and be responsible for, or canceling the whole thing. If they wouldn't do either, I'd ask to be relieved. I value my men's lives too much to do otherwise."

"Wow!" Ellis scratched his eyebrow, took his feet off of his desk and leaned toward Smith. "How is the last part of that going to help your men?"

"What do you mean?"

"Well, if you asked to be relieved, they'll just get another officer that's willing to follow their orders. Seems to me that you'd be a lot more tuned into trying to save your men's lives than somebody they'd get to replace you."

Smith looked shaken. He took a couple of deep breathes. "You're right. I hope I'm never faced with that."

Pete Ellis pulled the piece of paper from in front of Holland, wrote a word on it and shoved it back. It read, *Pacific*.

Holland glanced at the paper and nodded grimly. Pete Ellis was developing into one of the Marine Corps finest strategic thinkers and intelligence sleuths. Smith and he had spoken often about "what was next."

Ellis was convinced that two things would happen. That the war in Europe would rekindle again, the timing being the only thing unsure. The other was that US interests in Asia would come into so much conflict with the Japanese that war between the two countries was inevitable. He saw that happening in ten to fifteen years. Ellis also saw the coming Pacific war as a very difficult one. "Fighting out there on those islands will make a drinker out of you, just like me, Holland." Pete opened a desk drawer and removed a bottle of scotch. "Want a belt?"

"Too early for me, Pete." Holland couldn't help frowning. "You need to watch that stuff, it can sneak up on you."

"Oh, I'll keep my eye on it." Ellis held the bottle up in front of his face and stared at it in mock concern. He pulled the cork from its top and took a couple of swigs before wiping his mouth with the back of his hand. Pete placed the cork in the opening, pounded it in with the flat of his hand, and returned the scotch to its berth in his desk. "Believe me, Smitty, about the second or third island landing you're involved with, you'll be downing every drop of booze you can get your hands on."

"We'll be involved, no doubt of that." Holland nodded his agreement.

"Yep. You know what, most every one of those will be frontal assaults. How do you move to the flank on an atoll that's only a few square miles? How do you sneak up on an island that's hundreds of miles from your base on slow ships that air reconnaissance will spot two or three days before you arrive? You're only going to have a limited choice of landing beaches and the Japs will know which ones they are. They'll be dug in as good as the Kaiser's boys were. Worse still, sloshing through the surf over an open beach will make Flanders Fields look like heaven. Look what happened to our British friends at Gallipoli. Of the first two hundred men that landed at Cape Helles, only twelve made the beach alive. Most of their regiments had seventy percent casualty rates. I remember that the Dublin Fusiliers only had eleven men make it through the campaign out of 1012 that started. Think that would make you look for a bottle?"

"The British made a mess of the whole campaign, particularly the amphibious landing. They landed the bulk of the troops right under a Turkish fort. Their fleet lobbed a few shells at the defenders, but there was no coordination with the landing. Most of the soldiers came ashore in ships' longboats. The Turks slaughtered them even though the Ottomans were badly out-numbered at the landing beaches. Hell, the British and French lost over 44,000 killed and over 90,000 wounded in the nine months the campaign lasted."

"I agree Holland, the whole thing was bungled, but what I'm saying is we won't have a choice. If we go to war with Japan, we've got to go over 4,000 miles of the Pacific to get to their home islands. They have bases on atolls and islands all along the way to keep us from getting there. We have to take at least some of them if we have any hope of defeating Japan. That means we're going to have to make dozens of Galipollis. We'd better learn how to fight an amphibious war. We agree we can't afford the type of losses the British had. So, you'd better sharpen up all those ideas you have about landing Marines on an opposed beach because I believe you're going to be asked to do it."

3

Nature's War:
the Okeechobee Killer Hurricane
1928, South Bay, Florida

"I don't like the look of that, Cecil." A middle-aged woman stood on her front porch gazing critically at the low clouds moving in from the northeast. They were gray shrouds that reminded her of what she'd seen before.

Cecil Hartridge scratched his head. The intermittent showers were sure to make his bad situation worse. The near record rains of the previous six weeks had turned the fields he farmed into knee-deep mire. Muck soils surrounding Lake Okeechobee became black soup in very rainy conditions. Poking at his scrambled eggs and bacon he grumbled, "It ain't gonna make gettin' that damn tractor dug out and back to the shed any easier. I wanna get it protected just in case that storm does come a headin' this way."

"Do you think we ought to leave? Remember what happened over in Moore Haven two years ago. That storm killed 200 people and about wiped out the town."

Cecil hesitated between forkfuls of eggs. "I think we'll be okay. Last thing I hear tell was from the Rallie boy. He said he talked to someone up at Denton's store. The hurricane hit Puerto Rico and killed 275 there, but the radio report was that they didn't think it would hit Florida. We're a far piece from the lake and the dike. The house is built good even if it does hit here."

Ellen Hartridge didn't look convinced. "Cecil, when I went to Moore Haven to help, it was terrible. Half the houses was blowed down. The folks that made it through didn't have nothing to eat for a week." She pointed to the New River Canal which flowed within 100 yards of their home. "Look at those white caps. We're less than a half mile from the lake here. It could cut us off from South Bay. I sure wish we had a radio."

"If'n I don't keep this farm goin' and make my contracts, we ain't gonna have money to eat on, much less buy fancy stuff." Hartridge shoved the remainder of his breakfast to the center of the wooden table. "I'm gonna go by an' get Foozy an' his mules to jerk the tractor out. When Hister and Willie come up, send them out to meet me in the field. They know where the damn thing's stuck. Reckon I need to go into town to get ice after I get the tractor to the shed. I'll see if'n I can find out somethin'."

* * *

Ellen watched as her husband and their two black farm

hands piled out of the truck. Their faces were sober and concerned. Hister and Willie ran towards their houses a quarter mile away. Cecil lifted a box out of the truck bed containing ice blocks for their cooler. When he got to the porch stairs he said, "It's comin' this way. We need to get ready." As he passed he added, "Hear tell that the damn thing is headin' at West Palm Beach."

"Oh no!" Ellen said.

"Ed Forbes and his boys was a runnin' all over South Bay tellin' everybody they could to either get to a safe spot or get out. The storm's close to West Palm now."

"Are we going to get out of here? We aren't going to stay, are we?" Ellen clutched her husband's arm with frantic fingers.

"I'd like to, Ellen, but I don't think we'd have a chance of makin' it to any place safe. We wouldn't make it halfway to Clewiston on those farm trails. The truck would get stuck sure and we'd be caught out in it. I'm sure we couldn't make it to Palm Beach before the hurricane gets there. Those winds are already so strong, bein' outside in those gales would be suicide."

"What about going to Pahokee and up the Conner Road?" Fear had a firm grip on Ellen.

"I thought about doin' that. What if that storm goes over Okeechobee City? We'd be in as bad shape there. That's if'n we made it." Cecil shook his head. "I think we'd best do all we can here." He put his arm around his wife's shoulders. "We've got a right strong house. It's four foot off the ground. I can't imagine the water comin' that high, even if some of the lake comes over the dike. I'll board up the winders and reinforce everything I can in the time we got."

"When will it get here?"

"Old Ed said he reckoned sometime right after dark. Him being a boat captain an' all, I'd bet on what he holds. He said with the wind coming the way it is, he figures it's headin' right for the lake." Cecil decided not to tell his wife the lake level at South Bay was already two feet higher than two days earlier. South Bay itself was only five feet higher than the normal lake level. "Ed's telling everybody in South Bay that they should go to that big barge the Huffman Company has moored by the locks. Like to be 200 folks on it. If there is a problem there, the panic will kill as many as the storm. I didn't want to get into that and figured you wouldn't either."

Ellen nodded grimly.

"I told the boys to bring their wives and young 'ns over here. Those shacks of theirs won't take much of a blow. When he heard me tell that to Hister, Foozy done asked if'n he, his wife and her mother could stay with us. He says old Wilson won't let no Negroes in his house if'n they work for him or not, no matter what. I told Foozy it was okay."

"That's fine, Cecil." Ellen smiled and worried about what they would eat . . . after the storm passed.

As though reading her mind, he added, "They're bringin' what supplies they got to add to ours. Chances are if they leave them they'll just go to waste anyhow."

Ellen nodded, relieved.

The winds were gusting to forty miles per hour already. Cecil's thought was about how much time he would have to brace and board. It would be dark by eight. It was after two. If the boys got there soon . . . .

* * *

Cecil had nailed boards on the windows, did his best to brace spots on the roof and walls he felt were most vulnerable, and did what they considered was their greatest hope, prayed. Ed Forbes' guess as to when the storm would be near them was accurate. The hurricanes wrath began hitting them in the late afternoon. By six, Cecil estimated the winds were close to 100 miles per hour.

As the winds and rain intensified, the black women sang hymns and prayed while trying to keep their children from being any more terrorized than they already were. That was no small order for fear gripped the women. The buffeting from the shrieking gale shook the house and all knew the worst hadn't yet arrived. Ellen split her time between consoling their guests and being consoled by her husband. Cecil, Hister, Willie, and Foozy monitored the ceiling, walls, windows and doors for damage. They were ready to try to fix any breaches to their shelter with the boards and nails left over from what they had done outside.

The small cracks purposefully left between a few of the planks covering the windows allowed the house's occupants to peep on the attack nature was in the process of delivering outside their creaking, groaning shelter. Cecil heard a new sound and pressed his eye to one of the openings. It confirmed his fear. Water covered almost all the ground between their house and the New River Canal. Waves lapped at the lowest step of five. If the storm's eye wouldn't arrive until after dark, that meant . . . Cecil muttered, "Shit!"

"What's wrong?" Ellen asked. Her eyes were wide with alarm.

"Water's comin' up from the canal. Must be six inches coverin' most of the fields 'tween here and there." Between the overcast and the coming night it was difficult to see. As he stared out, a piece of debris zipped by his peep, banged against the column support for his front porch and disappeared into the gray sheets of horizontal rain.

The crash made by the debris caused Ellen to shout, "Ohhhh!!" and the black women and children to scream. Within seconds there was a louder cracking and grinding noise. Willie yelled from the back bedroom, "Mista Cecil, you done lost part a your roof!"

Cecil knew the rest would soon follow. If the roof was completely destroyed the rest of the house would quickly follow.

"It's a tearin' up more, Mista Cecil!"

The women were screaming and praying. Cecil Hartridge knew he'd made a mistake, one from which he and the people depending on him wouldn't recover. If there was any chance at all it would be to get to the Huffman Barge. That meant trying to make it there on foot in the teeth of the wind and blowing debris that could kill in an instant. He peered through the crack between the boards covering the window. Water now covered the second step. That meant a rise of around nine inches in less than a quarter hour. Rain couldn't account for that much flooding. It must be lake water topping the dike. Cecil's heart sunk. It would be suicide to try to make it to the barge.

"Oh, Lord!" Cecil couldn't tell who screamed, but in less than a second he knew why. Screeching, crackling preceded the final snaps of the last boards holding the roof in place. It flew off the house into the grayness that comes before full-fledged night. Wind and rain stung them as it invaded the house, trying to destroy the building and everyone inside.

"I'm needin' help!" Foozy yelled. He stood, leaning at an angle, pushing as hard as he could against one of the exterior walls which bulged inward. The roof and its framework took the house's rigidity with it. Cecil knew his friend's effort was futile. Within minutes the structure would be ripped to shreds. The question was whether or not there would be enough left to provide them something to cling to; the alternate would be walking or swimming to something strong enough to let them grasp it and pray they survived.

With a "bang" the front door was ripped from its hinges. One of the women screamed, "Aaahhh!" Cecil looked at what she saw as she pointed through the door. He saw a cow that half-walked and half-rolled in the water outside in his yard, a yard that had become part of Lake Okeechobee. It was unable to remain standing. One fact struck him immediately: Ellen couldn't swim. The water had risen another foot. He needed to find something to act as a raft if his wife was to survive.

Cecil removed his belt, turned their dining table over, strung it through holes in the supports, and fashioned into an improvised life preserver. He called to Ellen, "Come over here."

The terror in her eyes spoke more than words could.

"If we end up havin' to leave here or get blowed out, you stay with me. I'll see you get on the table." He pointed to his belt. "You hang on to that no matter what."

Ellen nodded. She grabbed his arm and asked, "Are we

going to die?"

Cecil thought of lying, but their condition was too obvious, so he said, "I don't know. All we can do is try our best and pray."

Within a few minutes one section of the wall whisked away. "Look after your families!" Cecil yelled to the other men. As he did so the faint screams of others somewhere out in the storm drifted to them. Many screams. Frantic screams. Death-laden screams. Cecil looked outside. His eyes followed the canal toward the lake. The Huffman Barge was outlined in the last vestige of light preceding total darkness. It was higher than the locks! That meant a wall of water, debris, and struggling screaming humans were hurtling toward them. It meant what little shelter they had would be swept away in a matter of seconds. He yelled, "Everyone grab somethin' that floats. The dikes busted and the lake'sa comin' right at us."

Cecil had time to see his wife kneeling on the table, clutching his belt with both hands, and the Negro women grasping their children. Water around his feet alerted him seconds before the surge of the wave struck the house. He heard screams all around him as the floor tilted, the remaining walls collapsed, and they were all thrown into the water. . . .

* * *

Bright skies and a light breeze covered the sawgrass marsh three miles south of Lake Okeechobee. Spread out in line, four men walked through the swamp, searching. They were fifty feet apart. One pulled a Jon boat through water that varied from knee to thigh deep. Tethered to the back of the boat by means of ropes were five bloated corpses that were dragging along behind. To protect the bodies, and in no small part the sensibilities of the men tasked with retrieving them, sheets and blankets covered the heads and upper bodies, the ropes that towed them behind the craft were tied around each victim's neck holding the make-shift shroud in place.

There was no disrespect for the dead intended. Besides being an unbelievably vile and abhorrent task, the searchers had long since learned that trying to lift the badly decomposing bodies into the boat simply wasn't practical. The flesh tore away, bloated abdomens burst, and the stench, already at unbearable levels, increased immensely. Besides, the boat was needed to cross waters too deep to wade through and to carry tools and supplies.

Two of the men wore blue overseas caps of the America Legion, an organization that was one of the primary responders to the disaster. They'd worked almost without sleep since they'd arrived three days after the storm. At first, they looked for survivors. Now, eight days after the storm, their task was to find the corpses of 2000 souls killed by the hurricane, many of which were yet to be found.

"You think any of them got carried this far?" asked one of the Legionnaires.

A black man that accompanied them spoke, "Dey found three folks down by da second locks. Dats near six miles from South Bay."

"How far in are we?" The other blue-capped man asked.

"Don't know." The black man looked at the fourth member of the search party. "Mista Elmer, what you think?"

The tall thin man shook his head. "Don't rightly know. Most all the trees and stuff that would let you know where you are . . . they're gone." He adjusted the bandage over his left eye and forehead. He looked around, searching for identifying landmarks. "Ain't for sure, but that there area looks like where Twenty-six Palms was. That'd mean we'd be three or so miles south of town." A local resident, he was serving as guide and trying to identify the bodies of his friends and neighbors. "They's been somebody this way." He pointed at something in the distance to their left. "See it?"

All three strained their eyes until each one saw the white rag tied to a support of some kind fluttering over the sawgrass. They all knew what it meant. It marked the location of a body someone had found, but had no means to remove.

"We aren't ever going to find them all," one of the American Legion men said. He'd been wading though sawgrass swamps, flooded agricultural fields, and custard apple thickets for six days and was near exhaustion. The volunteers that had been doing the grisly tasks were in need of replacements. "Let's go for another couple hours, then let's get all those we found out for the truck to pick up and bury."

The townsman said, "I don't think they're gonna bury most of them from now on. Ed Forbes told me them that aren't claimed right on or can't be identified are being burned."

They shook their heads and continued on. They'd waded two hundred yards when one of the Legionnaires yelled, "I see one." He sloshed twenty-five yards to his left and stared down through the grass into the water. The other men joined him. The corpse was bloated, it's eyes protruding, tongue out, and nearly naked. It was beginning to be hard to distinguish black from white at the stage decomposition had reached.

"I ain't sure, but I think dat's Cecil Hartridge. His house is gone and ain't no one seen none of his people since the storm." The black man took his floppy straw hat off in respect. "I sure do believe dat be Mista Hartridge."

"Yeh, I think you're right, Tom," the townsman agreed. "I'll fetch the boat and a blanket." He splashed off.

"What's he got in his hand?" one blue-capped man asked.

"It' a piece of board," the other Legionnaire said. He leaned over to examine it. "There's some kind of message scratched on it. Looks like, *Help. Ellen and Foo got broke legs. On tab.* I'd say he was going for help." The man straightened up. "This man survived the storm and evidently some folks were with him."

The black man shook his head sadly, "Ellen be his wife. Foo is probably Foozy. He's a friend of mine. Don't know who Tab be. They's probably dead by now."

"Good God, what a horrible way to die! To manage to live through the hell of a hurricane like that only to die because help can't get to you. They'd almost have been better off drowning." The Legionnaire removed his cap and wiped the perspiration from his brow . . . and the tears from his cheek. "What I saw in France on battlefields during the war was horrible, but in its own way, this is as bad if not worse."

"Dr. Buck, he say lots dem folks died 'cause dey be hurt but cain't get no help. He da doctor man in Belle Glade. He done fixed up lots a folks. He say dat der ain't enough supplies and he be needin' help, bad."

"Until they get the debris off the Palm Beach Road and the water goes down more, everything has to come in by small boat or tractor. Not a whole lot of relief supplies or rescue workers will make it in until they can be moved by truck. The Connor Road is washed out and part of it is still under three foot of water, so that's no help. The railroad won't have the grade rebuilt for months. Even if you got men and supplies to South Bay, would it help that much? You need some way to get to these people a lot faster than wading around in this swamp pulling boats."

"Ain't no way better I can think of," Tom said.

"You're probably right, but until there is, a lot of people are going to die every time this happens," the Legionnaire said.

"It's getting hard to pull this," the townsman said as he stopped the boat next to the body. "I think we might ought to mark him with a flag. We'll come back tomorrow or tell someone else—"

"I'll pull. And, I'll put a blanket on him and tie him up. I just can't leave the man here." The Legionnaire who had removed his hat, sighed before bending over the boat.

"I'll help," the black man volunteered.

"I reckon we all will." The townsman removed a length of rope from the boat.

"What about his wife and the other ones?" the other Legionnaire asked.

"Tomorrow," the townsman said. "Another day won't make no difference, now."

4

Planting a Seed – for a Machine . . . and a Man
1932, Don Roebling
John Roebling's Home, Lake Placid, Florida

John A. Roebling looked out his estate's window and watched the cool winter winds toss and twist the cabbage palms' fronds. Their movement was wild and reckless, without intent or purpose, like youth. Like his boy. Was their tortured movement an omen? He had an idea, one that would solve several problems including a very personal one posed by his son Donald. Constantly moving, aimless contorting, those leaves made no progress and were a graphic symbol of how he saw his child. The young man had recently married and needed to gain a focus in life. John hoped he'd thought of a means to accomplish that.

To the present, Roebling's son had taken full advantage of being an heir of one of the richest American families during the early 1900's. Wealth generated by August Roebling, builder of the Brooklyn Bridge, and expanded by John through his manufacturing and financial efforts, insured the boy's economic well-being. Donald's awareness of his fortunate situation allowed him to choose a life of self-centered indulgence, though he was not ungenerous to others.

John had hoped to launch his son into the world of responsibility by setting him up in the building business. The business did very well, but failed to accomplish the father's objective. Don "loosely" managed the luxury home construction company his father had financed for him. John's mistake: staffing the firm with good managers and foremen. Don delegated most responsibilities for running the company to his competent employees and continued doing as he pleased. He preferred spending his time tinkering with his hobbies: stamp collecting, HAM radio operation, and metal working.

Donald was a disappointment to his father. Roeblings were lions of the community; so far Don appeared to be a house cat. The boy wasn't bad, just very different—John preferred to think of him as eccentric. From an early age, Donald was addicted to candy and sweets. Since he avoided strenuous physical activity, he became obese at a very young age. Currently twenty-three, he carried much of his 400 pounds in his huge thighs and buttocks. The young man was blessed with natural intelligence, but had done little to enhance it.

Single-minded and temperamental as an adolescent, he grew up enjoying his wealth and its privileges with little responsibility and less discipline for balance. Hoping boarding school might help the youth, his parents sent

Donald to the Stuyvesant Prep School. His social style and appearance isolated and estranged him from his classmates. Other than reinforcing his independent and egocentric nature, little was accomplished by his attendance there. Don spurned the opportunity to attend engineering school at Rensselaer Polytechnic Institute, the school his father and grandfather had attended. At nineteen, Don chose to enroll in the Bliss Electrical Academy. John realized what was ahead when the school kicked Donald out due to constant conflicts with the teaching staff during his brief attendance there. Though Don's academic work was good, his vociferous contempt for his professors wasn't. Even John's suggestion that he might become the school's wealthiest patron, *if* his son could re-enroll, wasn't enough to make the administrators at Bliss reconsider. John thought, *yes, those writhing palm fronds were a perfect metaphor for his son's life to-date.*

Donald's return home proved a test for parents and child. A constant test of wills kept the Roebling's home-life in turmoil. Soon, Donald relocated to Clearwater, Florida, where he lived with a cousin. It was there his father helped Don establish his contracting business and where Donald built a magnificent mansion for him and his new wife. John hoped the business and marriage would settle Donald and introduce some seriousness into the twenty-three-year-olds mental makeup. So far, he saw no signs of that happening.

He didn't expect—

"Mr. Roebling."

John turned and stared across his parlor. Three of his long term employees stood, fidgeting uncomfortably, at the room's entrance. Billie Slater and his brother Zeb had worked for John since he first purchased property in Florida. Henry Watkins was his caretaker on Roebling's Lake Okeechobee properties. John smiled, waved, and said, "Come in, gentlemen."

They entered nervously. All three "Cracker" boys were far more comfortable on a tractor, in a pole shed or grubbing in the earth rather than entering a richly appointed, expensively furnished room; particularly if that room belonged to their boss.

John motioned to the chairs and couches. "Please, have a seat."

The three picked their seating carefully and sat down as though they had eggs in their pockets.

"Have you boys thought about what we discussed a couple days ago?"

"Yes sir, Mr. Roebling. We're all ready," Billie Slater said.

"Good! We're waiting on one person. Then we can get started."

"You really gonna try an' do this?" Billie asked.

"Definitely. I hope we can get one built before the '34

hurricane season."

"Who's buildin' it?"

"My son, Don."

The three men looked at each other, alarm in their faces. They directed their eyes to the floor. After a few seconds, Billie glanced at the other two before asking. "Are we gonna be workin' for him?"

"No. I just want you fellows to tell him about your experience in '28. You might have to drive him around the lake to see where the problems you've told to me about occurred."

All three men looked relieved. "We'll be glad to do anything we can to help." Billie relaxed, slumping lower in his chair. "It's sure a fine thing you're doin.' If we'd had a rescue machine like you was talkin' about the other day, we could a saved a bunch of them 1800 people that died down there."

"This will be a good project for Donald," Henry Watkins said. "He's really clever and sharp with mechanical stuff. It'll work out well with that machine shop he's building." He thought more like a manager than a field hand *and* he was perceptive. "We can show him what it has to do, but it's not going to be easy to build something that does what you're asking and have it hold together." Henry grinned. "It'll keep him real busy for a long while."

John's acknowledgment of Watkin's comments was

frosty. "That's true." Noting that the men's vision quickly returned to the floor after he rebuked Henry, he mitigated his mistake. "Look, fellows, let's be honest. I'd like to get Donald interested in something that will help him reach his potential. I don't expect him to build another Brooklyn Bridge like his grandfather did. But he has capabilities and I want him to use them. I'd like your help in getting him there."

"Mr. Roebling, have you talked to him about doin' this?" Billie asked.

"I've discussed building the rescue vehicle a couple of times and he was enthusiastic about pursuing the project. Your first hand accounts will motivate him even more. Donald does have a very compassionate, humanistic side." Roebling heard the door bell, tilted his head and looked at his watch. "That's probably him."

"Right on time," Billie observed.

"No, he's an hour late."

"It's not eleven yet, Mr. Roebling. That's what time you told us to be here."

"Yes, that's right." John smiled.

"Oh…"

John's maid's voice and a male's answer were followed by the sound of heavy footsteps. Donald Roebling appeared in the parlor archway. Young Don had attractive facial features. His Prussian heritage was evidenced by his high forehead. Don's prominent brows, medium brown hair, deep-set brown eyes, thin lips, and perfectly formed nose gave him an actor's good looks, if one ignored his body. Even though he was well over six feet tall and broad shoulbered, it was difficult to observe much about him other than his ponderous weight. The young Roebling's prodigious midsection, rear-end and thighs demanded so much attention the rest of his appearance dimmed to insignificance.

He smiled as he entered the room. "Hello, Dad. Hi, boys." He walked to the sofa where Henry Watkins was seated. "Henry, do you mind taking another seat? The chairs in here don't fit me well."

"No problem, Don." Henry smiled and rose, selecting another seat.

Donald's sitting in the sofa was reminiscent of a whale reentering the ocean after leaping. "Thanks. Say, boys, don't let me forget to give you some special chocolates I have specially made for me." He chuckled. "I guarantee you won't forget them."

"We appreciate it, Mr. Roebling," Billie said, acting as group spokesman.

"How's the quail hunting down on the ranch, Henry? If you can rig up a wagon to pull me in, I'm ready to give it another try," Don said.

"It's not good this year; the wet summer we had drowned out a lot of young birds. Your best bet would be your father's friend's pla—"

"I don't want to be rude, but I have another meeting this afternoon, so can we discuss what we came here for, the hurricane rescue vehicle." John's interruption produced a peeved look on Donald's face. Don held out one hand, palm up, towards his father and said, "Okay." Both father and son strove to control what was going on around them, creating friction between the two.

John cleared his throat and took charge. "I thought it would be good for you to hear the first hand accounts of what happened to Billie, Zeb and Henry during the '28 hurricane. I've also asked them to make suggestions about some essential features the craft needs. Fellows, I want Donald to get a picture of what those people went through. Who wants to start?"

"I guess I will," Billie said. "It ain't easy to talk about, though. Some of it was bad."

"Tell him just what you saw." John hoped Billie would make it challenging. The more catastrophic, the surer John was that Don would be captivated by attempting the daunting task.

"Okay." Billie faced Roebling's son. "Don, you know your dad sent us to see what we could do to help after the storm. We got down to Okeechobee City okay to meet up with Henry. That town was messed up and we could've helped there, but everybody said it was down south where they needed us. The people on the lake's north side got hurt some, but there aren't hardly any folks livin' there. Because of where the hurricane's eye went across the state, the south side got beat up bad. The wind got up close to 150 mph and blew the lake water out onto all those south shore towns. South Bay, Belle Glade, Pelican Bay and all the rest got washed away. Three things made it worse. First, the storm hit September 16th, that's toward the end of the rainy season, so the area was already half-flooded. There's not twelve feet of change in elevation anywhere south of the lake. And there was ten inches of rain that came with the storm. Second, most of those folks livin' there was Yankees. A bunch of them damn Miami land speculators sold the property by tellin' those folks the floodin' problem had been resolved. Most of them didn't know no better than to build their houses close to the ground, right where floodin' could ruin everything they owned and kill the people along with it. Anyway, the hurricane put up to eight foot of water over everything down there durin' the height of the storm. Last thing was that damned dike they was relyin' on. It was just eight feet tall and made of muck. Water got up to the top of it, and once it started over, the whole thing turned to mush. When it gave way it sent eight to ten foot a water washing out everything in front of it."

Billie shifted in his seat uncomfortably. "When we tried gettin' there, it was a real mess. We couldn't use the trucks like we wanted. The Connor road was washed out in places and it was covered with trees and parts of buildings, animals and dead folks. Every trail going to that part of the Lake had enough water coverin' it at one place or another that you couldn't get through. There ain't nothing but farm ruts from Clewiston east. Only way to get there was from West Palm. Most of the bridges were gone. Part of that road was still covered, too. Henry got us two boats, but we really couldn't use them much."

"Why?" Don asked. "I thought you said there was eight feet of water over the area."

"Most of the water ran back into the lake within twenty-four hours after the storm passed. It left the land in conditions that varied from soggy mud to being covered with a few feet of water, dependin' on the land contours. It took us a day-and-a-half just to get down to where South Bay had stood. They was only a couple buildings left standing there. You'd drive a piece, have to build some type of temporary bridge or wait for the water to go down, get stuck in the muck and have to push out, or do a little searchin' with the boat. You'd see a house, or what was left of one, out in a field. A few times we'd see suspicious things layin' out in the pastures that we'd go investigate." Billie looked out the window so it was more difficult for the others to see his eyes. "Sometimes it was a dead cow or animal; sometimes it was just trash; once-in-a-while it would be a body. Water and heat ain't kind to dead folks." He looked down. "We brought the first couple back to the road, but it was obvious there was goin' to be too many of them. It was more important for us to get the food and relief supplies we were carryin' to the livin'. We didn't have a way to haul and handle bodies, so we moved them to the road or a high spot of ground, covered them best we could, marked the grave, and made a log of where they were so somebody could get them later. That was the best we could do. The heat and wild animals were too bad to just leave them. We gave the log to the sheriff's department, but I don't know if they ever picked them all up."

"Were you the only people trying to help?' Donald was becoming fully absorbed by the story.

"Oh, no!" Billie said. "There were people from around here, Fort Myers, Okeechobee City, and later on, from Miami and Tampa, all doin' their best. Even Tallahassee. The sheriff and county people helped too, but they were busy tryin' to keep order, get roads open, bridges up, and utilities workin'. Supplies were piled up on the road goin' to the Lake. That was so frustratin'. You couldn't get in to help the people, get supplies to them, or get the trapped folks out. There were a lot of people caught in the initial flood and they drowned outright. But I bet more than half that died lost their lives after the storm. They got up in trees, on roof tops, anyplace they could find to get out of the flood.

Many got washed miles back into the sawgrass. When the lake went down, lots died because they were injured and didn't get help soon enough, they didn't have food or drinkin' water, or died trying to get out on their own."

"Don't forget the damned snakes," Zeb said. "That was one of the worst things for them folks."

Billie shook his head and shivered. "The moccasins and rattlesnakes got washed out of the fields and swamps. They were lookin' for places to crawl out of the water. Unfortunately, there weren't many places to go around. The snakes, and there were a lot of them, got up on the same roof tops and trees those poor folks were on. A lot of people died of bein' snake bit."

Zeb grimaced. "It was bad. We'd been down there four days when we come across this family stranded on the top of a pole barn. Billie and I took a boat out to get them off. The father and two children were alive. The mother and a little six year old girl were bit by snakes and had died. We couldn't get the father to put the little girl down even after we got him back to the road. If we could have gotten to them quick enough and to a doctor . . . well . . . . Hundreds of things like that happened. If we'd had something like your father's talkin' about, most of those people could have been saved. You just couldn't get around. Wheeled vehicles would get stuck and weren't of much use except on the only road that was open. Boats would get you from one point to another. Then you'd need land transport. You needed some kind of boat with wheels like what's on a tractor."

Donald leaned forward on the sofa. "It sounds like you need some kind of barge that's self-propelled with wheels and a propeller. Whatever we build will have to have lots of space to carry supplies in and people out. What was the biggest problem? Water too deep to drive a vehicle, or was it too muddy to keep from getting bogged down, or not having enough cleared land you could drive on?"

Henry said, "It was about equal. I mean, if you can't do all three of those things you'd have too many places you couldn't go. You could be driving along and get to a place that's underwater. If there's enough high ground to go around it's probably covered with Palmetto or some other scrub. Besides, most of that area is muck. It turns to black soup when it gets soaked. Wham! that quick you're down to the axle. If you're in a boat, a lot of the water is too shallow to run a motor on. There's so much trash and debris in the water it's hard to keep a prop in one piece. Then there are dikes along canals and elevated farm roads. If you're in a boat big enough to do any good, you may have to go miles to get around them. Even if the boat is small, the sides of those dikes and roads are steep and its backbreaking work to get a boat pulled across. If we'd had a vehicle that could be made to go through all those conditions, we could have saved hundreds of people. Honestly, I *don't* think you can design and make such a thing."

"Father, do you have something I can make some notes on?" Don asked.

"Sure." John Roebling rose from his chair, walked to a huge wooden desk and smiled as he removed a notepad and pencils. He'd seen that look on his son's face before. Donald Roebling liked nothing better than proving others wrong and doing what people believed impossible. Succeed or fail, the challenge had been accepted and the willful twenty-three year- old was committed.

* * *

"It's too late in 1932 for this season, or probably next, '34 is more realistic," said philanthropic humanist, John Roebling. "I'll pay all the design, development and production costs for you Donald. It's up to you to invent a commercially viable amphibious rescue vehicle." The father and son sealed the deal with a handshake. The elder Roebling's agreement to finance the project came with his most repeated admonition. "Son, the Roeblings, like all other patriotic Americans, owe a debt of gratitude to this country that has been so generous to us. We more than most. Remember that." With a nod of his head, the younger Roebling willing accepted and reaffirmed the caveat and held it sacred throughout his life.

* * *

Don immediately started his quest to build an amphibious machine that would fulfill all the rigorous requirements his father's employees had identified. It would consume the bulk of Donald's waking efforts for the next eight years giving shape and purpose to his life—a life that sometime bordered on the bizarre. Truly, young Roebling listened to music not heard by others. For example, the special chocolates made for Donald Roebling had chewing tobacco in their centers. Though many might question the sanity of Don Roebling actions, no one ever questioned the size of his heart's goodness. His kind generosity was as remarkable as his body's extraordinary bulk. His willingness to use his wealth to assist others and his desire to improve the human condition was a life-long trait.

Henry Watkins words about saving many human lives proved to be prophetic, *but* not at all as he had envisioned. Roebling's machine would save those lives because of another man's unflinching devotion to his profession which was killing, not sparing, his fellow man.

5

A New "Science"
1932, Holland Smith
Oahu, Hawaii

Six bored naval officers stood at the battleship's rail watching the mock amphibious landing. The beautiful blue water, swaying palm trees, crashing surf and white sand looked more appropriate for a vacationer's post card scene than a setting for a serious military training mission. The Navy men had completed their portion of the practice landing when the cruisers, destroyers and battleship had fired a few salvos from their big guns, simulating a pre-landing bombardment to soften the imaginary defending forces. Their biggest question—when would the exercise be complete, so they could enjoy Pearl Harbor's tropical playground? Impatience and exasperation covered their faces.

"Look at that mess! I firmly believe this is an exercise in futility—pure folly. I'm surprised old man Schofield sanctioned this circus." A nattily dressed naval captain pointed to the gaggle of small craft milling about, 5000 yards off shore. As the officers watched, some of the group's boats formed a wide arc as a prelude for their trip to the beach. The arc was necessary since every motor launch towed a standard un-powered ship's boat. Each miniature convoy was packed with Marines dressed in full battle gear. After the first group was aligned and on its way to the sand, a second formation made the same laborious turn. More groups were forming, readying themselves for the turtle race to the beach.

A lieutenant commander asked, "Why are they going in like that? Why not just get them in all at one time?"

"They'd be too hard to kill. In fairness to the enemy, the Marines attack in what they call waves. That gives whoever is shooting at them, more time to line up their shots," a wise cracking ensign offered.

The captain shook his head. "They should listen to what old Admiral Sims said about trying landings with those mud soldiers. He was running the Naval War College at Newport, when I attended back in '21. Sims knows what Marines are good for: guard duty at embassies, minor skirmishes ashore, ceremonies and custodial duties. He believed they didn't have leadership that can handle a big amphibious landing. Besides, if there was one important thing we learned from the British during World War I, it was that amphibious landings aren't practical—if not downright impossible. We studied Gallipoli at Newport. Talk about a disaster. Ask yourself if you'd want to jump out of a boat, wade to shore and run over a beach that is covered with fire from machine guns, artillery, mortars and snipers?!"

"Why, you'd have to be pretty stupid to want to do that." The ensign faked an enlightened expression. "Stupid? Stupid! Isn't that a qualification for being a Marine?"

The group laughed.

"You might not *want* to, but what if you *have* to?" Another one of the officer group, one wearing a commander's insignia, stared straight into the captain's eyes. "My understanding is that's exactly what we might be doing. The whole idea of this exercise is to be ready if we have to go to war with the Japanese. The war plan's core we're testing is to drive across the Central Pacific, seizing bases from the Japs to let us get close enough to attack their homeland. That means capturing a string of islands all the way to Japan. Most of those are tiny atolls and are hundreds of miles from anything else."

The captain snorted, "The Pete Ellis thing?"

The commander nodded. "When you have to attack a little strip of sand, there's no room for maneuver, the only way to do it is an over-the-beach frontal assault. Seems to me we should take what we're doing here very seriously. Rear Admiral Plunkett was at Newport at the same time Sims was there. He had a completely different opinion of the Marines and what they're capable of."

The captain answered coldly, "I didn't know you'd been to Newport."

"I haven't. But, I was in Plunkett's staff, the clerical group, before I got promoted. I've prepared a lot of his notes and correspondence. In fact, I've talked to him about what he sees as a major change in the coming war." The commander leaned against the rail. He had a smug smile on his face. "We're going to be fighting with Japan sooner or later. Since the Japs beat up Russia in 1906, and the Japanese thought old Teddy Roosevelt cut them out of some spoils they should have gotten, the US and Japan have been on a collision path. Maybe it will be in China, or the East Indies, but it will come. Why do you think the war plan exists? It's because the brass thinks there is a good chance that we'll end up fighting them. And why do you think so many of the top brass are here to see this? It may not be too long before we're at war with the Japs."

"The plan is there for the same reason any peace-time military plan exists, it's prudent to be ready to fight any and all of your potential enemies." The captain was clearly aggravated. "There's a plan to go back into Germany, if that would ever be a problem again, which it won't. It's more likely we'll be fighting in Mexico than fighting Japan. If we do go to war with the Japanese, we already have bases in the Philippines, Wake Island, Guam and Midway. It will be the big boys, the battleships, sailing from those bases that will decide who wins, *if* it ever comes to war with Japan." He waved derisively toward the shore. "You can bet that if it does boil down to an island hopping battle, it will be the Army, not the mud Marines, doing the fighting. We're wasting our time here. We should be back in Honolulu lining up the wahines."

The commander snorted and shook his head. "You need to take this more serious and forget about chasing hula girls."

The rest of the group chuckled and the captain's face reddened. "I know some guy on MacArthur's staff." The captain searched his pockets for a cigarette, found an empty pack, wadded it up and disgustedly tossed it over the rail. "Old Doug's pushing to get the Marines disbanded. Fighting land battles are what the Army is for. With the depression making money tight, MacArthur says it's a waste of funds to have what amounts to a duplicate force. He wants the money congress would authorize for the Marine Corps. A lot of the Navy brass agree with him. Want to bet he doesn't get it?"

"What do you want to lose?" The commander turned and pointed to an officer standing at the rail 150 feet away from the group. The man wore a Marine uniform complete with a lieutenant colonel's insignia. He was peering through a pair of binoculars, watching the mock landing intently. "That guy is one of the men that have been pushing hard for expanding the Marines and making it a major part of naval operations. In fact, he advocates that Marine, not Navy, officers command invasion operations. There's a core of people like him. Major General John Russell is commandant of the Marines and I know he's working hard to get a Fleet Marine Force authorized."

"Who's your friend down the rail?" One of the other officers asked.

"Holland Smith. He's an acquaintance, not a friend. He's serving here on the *California* as Marine Battle Force Officer and reports to Admiral Schofield."

The captain stiffened. "Howlin' Mad Smith?"

"The same."

"I've heard about him. He's got the reputation of being opinionated, hot-tempered and difficult. One of my Annapolis classmates has had dealings with him. Says his fuse is so short you can't find it. I also know he's not afraid to buck the Navy big-shots when it comes to something he feels strongly about. Smith attended the Naval War College a few months before I was there. Some of the arguments Sims and Smith had really caused a stir. Holland Smith kept putting forward ideas to include Marine Corps troops in written battle plans. Like I said, Sims had a low opinion of the Marines and freely expressed it. As I heard it, the two were at each others throats. One of my friends was there. He said Smith came as close to insubordination as you can get without a court-martial." The captain cocked his head to the side. "But he ended up getting the Marines written into a battle plan for the first time in Navy history. You know Chet Nimitz; well, he told me about him. Nimitz had a skirmish with him. He says besides being a wildcat, he's also an intelligent and hard working officer. I'm curious. Think you could introduce me?"

"I've only met him a couple times, but sure." The commander looked at the other four men in the group. "You fellows want to come along?" The invitation was greeted with grunted "no's" and head-shakes.

The Marine officer they approached was a man of average height and build. His hair was tinged with gray and he appeared to be in his late forties. Behind the binoculars he pressed to his eyes, the Marine hid an intense scowl. He held a note pad and pencil in his other hand.

As the two officers stopped next to the Marine, their right hands snapped up to their brows. The commander said respectfully, "Colonel Smith, sir, I have someone who'd like to meet you."

The man swiveled his head around, he snapped off a quick return salute, and said in a voice that carried the remnant of a southern accent, "Ah, Gentry, the last time we met you were a lieutenant; congratulations." Smith's head turned and he peeked through the binoculars. "I hope you gentlemen will understand this exercise is very important to me." As he pivoted around, he stuck his binoculars under his left arm, then extended his hand to the captain, saying,

"Lieutenant Colonel Holland Smith. That's Holland like the country."

"Captain Fred Wilson. Pleased to know you. We have a mutual acquaintance, Chester Nimitz. He's told me a lot about you." The captain smiled as he took Smith's hand and shook it.

"I only met Nimitz a few times, but he seemed like a good man. All Texan." Smith sneaked a peek at the landing craft. "Excuse me." He dropped Wilson's hand and snatched the binoculars from beneath his arm pit. He quickly aimed them at the flotilla crawling toward the shore. When he found the first wave he exclaimed, "Shit!" He returned the field glasses to their temporary storage space under his arm. Smith scrawled two lines of notes on the pad and slapped the binoculars back to his face. "They can't get out of formation that far. They'll swamp or capsize the towed boats in the wake. Bastards!" He peered through the glasses. "Damn it, one of the boats broke loose and it's adrift." The lieutenant colonel shook his head and said several unintelligible words. His binoculars made another trip to temporary storage; he wrote more notes before he returned the field glassed to his eyes. The frown lines on Smith's face were deeply etched. He renewed his intense vigil.

"What did he have to say?" Smith said.

"Who?" The two officers asked simultaneously.

The Marine never took the field glasses down, nor was there the slightest change in his expression. "Nimitz."

Captain Wilson answered truthfully. "He said that you're a very good officer, that you work hard, are intelligent, know and love the Marine Corps like no one else he knows, but you can be, I think the word he used was, 'cantankerous,' sir."

Smith's expression never changed and his concentration on the events unfolding at the shoreline never wavered. "Chet was being diplomatic. He usually is. I'm a real pain in the ass if I believe I'm correct and the other guy's wrong. That doesn't mean I'm right all the time; it means I don't give up easy. But, I am most of the—oh, shit!" He continued to watch the first wave as it got nearer the beach. "I knew it, I knew it." Smith duplicated his routine and scribbled a few more sentences. Without looking at the two men at his side he said harshly, "Gentlemen, as I said, this mock landing is very important. I need to keep my full attention on what's going on. If ya'll will excuse me." Short of asking Wilson and Gentry to leave, Smith made it clear he wanted to be left alone to observe the landing.

After platitudes and a quick parting salute, the two officers returned to their group still standing at the rail 150 feet away.

"Well?" one of the officers asked as Wilson and Gentry rejoined them.

"He seems alright, but a hard-ass," Wilson offered. He grinned, "He was so immersed in what's going on out there that we didn't get much out of him. You'd have to expect that with his troops going in. And I don't think he was happy with how things were going." He turned to Commander Gentry. "You know more about him than any of us. What's his background and what's the scuttle-butt?"

"I told you I don't know him that well, but I'll tell you what I've heard." Commander Gentry glanced at Smith who was busy writing more comments on his note book. "Smith's from the South and a military tradition. He's been in the Corp since 1906, at least, that's when he was commissioned as a 2nd lieutenant. It's said he was offered a chance to go to West Point, but his parents made him turn it down. Not sure why. Anyway, I know he went to Alabama Poly and later graduated from the University of Alabama's law school."

"Hallelujah, an unreconstructed Rebel. That's wild, a Marine with a lawyer's mind. Will wonders never cease," the ensign cracked. "I'll bet there aren't many in the Marines. Hell, he may be the only one. Is that what he's done, spent his time in the Judge Advocate's office?"

"No! He's seen all kinds of action. I know he's done sea duty several times. He was in the Philippines, Nicaragua, Panama, China, Santo Domingo, fought in France and was assigned to Pershing's staff during the war. Since then he's had several training commands and has been at the forefront in developing amphibious warfare. Plunkett told me Smith served with Pete Ellis when they were in France with the 4th Brigade. That's who—"

One of the officers interrupted Gentry, "Ellis? You mentioned him earlier. Who is Pete Ellis? I know I've heard his name before, but I can't remember what it was connected to."

Gentry finished his sentence. "That's who originated most of the Pacific war plans against Japan. Pete Ellis was a brilliant strategist, one of our best. After the war in Europe, he turned his attention to the Japanese when they started fortifying the islands that were mandated to them. His plan is the one we're still working from today. He was given a special 'leave' to wander through the Pacific islands. Ellis tried to get on to the ones the Japs controlled to test his theories. The last place he went was Palau in the Carolines. He died there . . . mysteriously. The Japanese said he drank himself to death. That could be right—he was probably poisoned because they knew he was gathering intelligence. We sent a chief pharmacist mate to get the body and investigate. He came back with Ellis' cremated ashes and an incoherent story about what happened to Pete. Strange, the mate and his wife died shortly afterwards in a Tokyo earthquake. You believe in coincidences? We'll never really know what happened to Ellis."

One of the officers looked at his watch. "Gentlemen, let's go to the mess hall. It's getting close to lunch. There's not a damn thing we can do here."

The group all nodded and meandered toward the officer's mess. As they were walking, Wilson asked Gentry, "I wonder why Smith isn't on the bridge with all the big brass? I know Schofield and at least a half dozen admirals and generals are up there."

"Probably doesn't want the interruptions. He can rid himself of guys like you and I a lot easier than those wearing stars. I think rubbing elbows with the Navy higher-ups isn't on Howlin' Mad's list of favorite things." Gentry knew, but purposely didn't say, that was a major understatement.

* * *

Holland Smith sat in his cabin reviewing the notes he'd made as he observed the combined exercises designed to test the Navy and Marine's strength, skill and knowledge in amphibious warfare. He wondered if the Navy's upper echelons were as dismayed as he was by what had transpired and what they'd witnessed during the last couple days. It was clear that the training the Marines had was inadequate. There was a lack of coordination between naval gunfire support and aerial bombardment with the assault forces, and most importantly, a complete lack of the proper equipment to attempt a landing on a hostile beach.

The Marines landed in standard ship's boats. These craft were unable to cross the reef at many places. Those assigned a landing lane where the reef barred the way had to scramble to find a place to pass through. This mayhem completely destroyed the timing and even distribution required to land troops. Once the boats cleared the reef, the powered units had trouble in the surf. Some foundered or capsized as the men piled out into the water and waded laboriously to the sand. If a powered craft made it to land, after unloading, most boats couldn't get off the beach. The towed boats had trouble when the powered units had to zigzag to find passages through the reef. Many cut loose and rowed to shore. Smith visualized enemy machine gunners licking their lips as the frail boats approached the surf. Most made it to the beach but were abandoned by their crews since the powered boats that successfully backed off the sands were unable to maneuver to take the towed units back with them. Soon the landing area was jammed with boats, materials and confused men. There was no place for the later waves to come ashore in a coordinated attack. They drifted toward the crowded sands desperately looking for landing space. It took four times as long as it should to assemble sufficient manpower to launch the attack. If it had been an actual landing, it would have been a bloody catastrophe.

Smith shook his head and muttered, "If the Japs had been holding that island, we couldn't have captured it." He thought for a few more seconds before adding, "In fact, we couldn't have landed at all." He turned the pages of his note pad until he reached a clean sheet. Smith wrote the heading on the page's top: "Critical items needed to make amphibious assaults doable." The first item his pencil scrawled on the paper was, "#1 – Development of a shallow draft landing craft that can cross reefs and go up onto the beach, unload, and then retract itself. If possible, it needs to be armored and amphibious." Smith underlined the whole passage, double underlining the last sentence.

6

Searching for a Solution
1934, Holland Smith
Marine Corp Barracks, Washington DC

"I'd like you to meet Andrew Higgins. Mr. Higgins has a boat design which I thought might interest you. I'm hoping we'll spend time discussing it at this morning's meeting." The navy lieutenant looked at the man standing next to him, then at the Marine. "Mr. Higgins, this is Lieutenant Colonel Holland Smith. He's involved in developing amphibious warfare."

Smith extended his hand to the man whose Irish heritage was plainly visible in his features and personage. Higgins took Smith's hand and they exchanged a firm hand shake, each sensing the strength in the other and liking that chemistry.

"It's a pleasure to meet you Colonel Smith. Lieutenant Goddard, here, has told me a lot about you," Higgins said. "He tells me you're more open-minded than a lot of the Navy people I've been dealing with at the Bureau of Ships. Those folks are adverse to new ideas."

"It's Lieutenant Colonel. Hopefully, someday." Holland grinned. "I like you already. Anyone who has problems with those jackasses has got to be alright." Smith swiveled his head, nodding at the lieutenant. "You're not like those . . . *folks* . . . at the Bureau. Goddard, you should have been a Marine. Sure you don't want to transfer? We can use good men like you."

The lieutenant laughed. "I appreciate the compliment and the offer, but I think I'll stay where I'm at. You guys play too rough for me." Goddard made a quick survey of the hall where they stood. "Is there someplace we can talk privately for a few minutes?"

"Sure. My foxhole is a couple doors down. Follow me." Smith led the way into his office, requested his guests be seated as he settled behind his desk, then asked, "Okay, Lieutenant, why the need for privacy?"

"Honestly . . . there are background facts I thought you should know before 1100. Some Bureau people that will be sitting in the meeting don't share my opinion and might not like me informing you about Higgins' craft. It's important, or at least I think it's important, for you to know about it. The concept has many of the features you're wanting in a landing craft. I know you're not *directly* in the chain on this, but . . . ." Goddard winked.

Holland Smith raised one eyebrow and tilted his head to one side. "That's a nice way of sayin' you'd get your ass kicked by your brass if you brought the information up at the conference, right?"

"Kind of." Goddard took a deep breath. "I just thought you sh—"

"He knows a good product when he sees it," Higgins interrupted. "The Eureka, built in a proper configuration, is what Goddard tells me you've been looking for in a landing craft; one that works. Unfortunately, if you aren't connected with the firms the Bureau has been dealing with, good ideas don't mean anything."

"What in the hell is the Eureka?"

"It's a shallow draft boat that Mr. Higgins designed for use on the Mississippi and in the bayou country of Louisiana and the Gulf Coast. He sells the boat to companies that want to pick up and deliver materials, crews, anything, to locations where no dock facilities exist. I know what you've been looking for. I think it's very close." Goddard looked at Andrew. "Will you show him those photos and specifications, Mr. Higgins?"

"Absolutely!" Higgins removed a three-ring binder from his briefcase and placed it in front of Holland Smith. He opened the binder to a boat photo that looked like a powered barge. Twenty men stood in its spacious open interior. A small tractor and a pile of equipment shared the deck space with the human cargo. The boat's pilot sat in the stern portion of the boat.

"Damn. That looks good!" Holland Smith turned the page. The next picture showed the boat's bow resting on a

river bank as people loaded logs onto the craft. Smith whistled and said, "Is this a prototype or a production boat?"

"I've built quite a few of these. Before I closed it down,
I had a logging and lumber operation and used these boats
to move material. That's what I designed them for. See how
the bow can actually go right up on the bank? I call it a
'spoon' design. If you have two feet of water you can take
these boats anywhere and unload. You can back right off
the bank when you're done." Higgins turned a couple of
pages to a blueprint. "See this?" He pointed to a feature on
the drawing. "The propeller is housed in this tunnel. Anything the Eureka's bottom will pass over won't destroy the
blades on the prop. Logs, rocks, wreckage, anything."

Smith looked at the drawing with intense interest. The
hull tapered away from the boat's bow that required only
inches of draft to an almost flat bottom section that housed
the tunnel. It was a broad-beamed craft; no space was
wasted in the bow or stern design. The boat was truly a motorized barge. Holland asked, "What's it made out of?"

"Plywood." Higgins quickly added, "It could be armored or made from light steel plating."

"How thick of plating?"

"Twelve gage. Maybe a little heavier. If you make the
boat too heavy, it will be impossible to get the bow on the
beach and off when you're done. It will add a little to the
water it draws. Probably another nine inches. The added

weight will reduce its speed unless you increase the engine size. And then it's possible it won't maneuver as well. The Eureka handles surprisingly good, given the capabilities she has for hauling heavy loads. I know what you want the craft to do. I think your best bet would be to put light armor on the bow and where the coxswain will drive the boat."

Holland nodded. "How fast does she go?"

"I've built versions with speeds from eight to fourteen knots. The boat pictured is a forty-footer; its speed is twelve knots with a full load." Higgins turned a couple pages backward to a photo showing the craft with its nose nestled on a sand beach, waves pounding around the boat. "The Eureka handles adverse surf conditions quite well."

"When can we get one of these to test?" Smith asked. His enthusiasm was evident.

Goddard and Higgins looked at each other. "That's the problem," Goddard said. "And, it's the reason I pulled you in here before the meeting. My boss says we can't get *any* money appropriated for testing *this boat*. The depression has cut our budget for research to practically nothing."

"What do you mean by emphasizing the words *this boat*?" Smith asked.

"He means there is money in the budget, but the powers running the Bureau of Ships already has it allocated to *other manufacturers*," Higgins said. His last words were derisive.

"Someone's friends? Damn, we'll have to see if we can push to change that!" Holland's legendary temper began to rise. "I can't believe those brass hat bastards aren't moving on this. They know how bad we need a good landing craft."

"To be blunt, Lieutenant Colonel Smith, we're here because we need someone with a big enough set of balls to get a change made." Higgins slapped the binder closed. "I've tried for a while and I haven't been able to get anyone except Goddard here to back the purchase of one of my craft for *your* troops to test."

"What do you mean you've tried for a while?" Smith's voice became shriller and louder as his anger increased. His face reddened and his features showed the displeasure welling in him.

"Holland, Mr. Higgins has been offering this boat design to the Navy since 1927." Goddard looked at Smith pleading for assistance. "That's another reason why we think we need your help. I couldn't believe it when I took over my duties and found out how long this boat has been available to us. Sir, there are some lower level staff personnel in our office that realize the potential this craft has, but unfortunately the old time 'black shoe' salts have all the say. The only way Mr. Higgins is going to get a chance to show what his boat will do is if someone like you pushes for it. Pushes really hard."

"Well you've got that!" Smith growled. "Damned bastards!"

Goddard looked alarmed. "I hope you'll be diplomatic. I could . . ."

Smith held his hand up and said, "Lieutenant, don't worry, I'm not going to do anything that will get your butt chewed. As bad as I'd like to ream those bastards at the Bureau, I won't. Besides, I know the Navy way. If I cause too many waves, we'll never get a chance at the . . ." he glanced at the name on Higgins' binder, "Eureka." He shouted at another door leading from his office. "Hey, Fred, come in here."

A clerk appeared at the door. "Yes, sir?"

"Come look at this," Smith said. He pointed at the binder as Higgins laid it on Holland's desk. "Open it up, Fred."

The corporal opened the notebook to the first page. A large photo of the boat and its name were printed on the paper. "Yes, sir, what do you want me to do?"

"What is that a picture of and what is it called?" Smith pointed to the photo.

Fred looked confused, but said, "It's a boat and it's called the Eureka."

"Did you see this book lying on a desk *somewhere* and just happen to look in it?" Smith asked, winking at his clerk as he spoke.

Fred smiled and nodded. "Yes, sir."

"And you told me what you saw, didn't you?"

"Yes, sir!"

"Thanks, Fred, that's all." The clerk left the room suppressing a laugh at the door.

Goddard looked relieved.

"I can't believe it's taken this long for someone to show this to us." Smith's ire remained. "This craft does everything we want except go over reefs and drive itself up the beach. I don't guess you could modify the Eureka to do that, Mr. Higgins?"

"No. That's out of my competence area. You'll have to get someone else for that."

"Well, you have my complete support on this. I'll keep pushing until we get approval."

Holland Smith's face was determined.

"Thank you, Holland," Andrew Higgins said, "The Eureka will do a great job for you, I'm sure of it. I hope I can return the favor for you someday."

* * *

Holland Smith looked at the brief letter telling him that the Marines' request to fund purchasing one of Andrew Higgins landing craft hadn't been approved. It was signed by Lieutenant Goddard. A hand written note written on the bottom said, "Sorry, I couldn't get it in. Your help did keep the Eureka listed as a future possibility. I'll keep trying." Smith looked at the list of addressees. Most were Navy personnel in the Bureau of Ships. Holland growled, "I bet these people are celebrating."

He looked up a phone number, placed a call, and impatiently tapped his fingers on the top of his desk. "Lieutenant Sam Goddard, please," he requested. When a voice answered, Holland grunted his okay. As Smith waited, he looked at the memo as though it was a soiled diaper.

"Hello, Goddard, Holland Smith. I'm living up to my nickname right now. I am Howlin' Mad. I got your letter about the Eureka. What can I do to get some money authorized for Higgins' landing craft?" Smith listened. As Goddard spoke, Holland's face progressively twisted into rage as the lieutenant told his story. When Goddard finished, Smith exploded, "That's pure bull crap! Why can't we get a chance to try what *we* want? It would be one thing if there was *no* money allocated, but they're going to spend what little that is available on some wild—well, the whole thing stinks. I'm going to write the Marine Equipment Board and ask them to press the Bureau of Ships to get one of Higgins' boats for a test. And I want to write a letter to the brass in the Bureau to protest. They've furnished us a bunch of unseaworthy skiffs, Coast Guard boats, Cape Cod fishing boats, hell they even sent us boats confiscated from rum runners working the Florida coast. They might be great for smuggling booze, but they're not worth a damn for what we need. They need to listen to us, not some congressman trying to drum up business for people in his district. Who should I write to get action?"

Smith's face scowled as he wrote several names on a piece of paper. "Don't worry, I'm not going to do anything that'll get those assholes any madder at you than they are now. I appreciate what you're trying to do. One other thing, do you have Andrew Higgins' phone number? I have his business card here somewhere, but I can't lay my hands on it right now. I want to call him. Now. The Marines have a very strong interest in his boat and I want him to know we're not the problem in getting a damned order pushed through."

* * *

"Ada, it never ceases to amaze me. The Navy big-wigs refuse to listen to what we say about *our* needs in the Corps." Holland Smith swished his fork through the peas on his plate without scooping any up. "Today I wrote a letter asking those idiots in the Bureau of Ships to reconsider their rejection of the best landing craft I've heard about. I told you about that man Higgins' Eureka boat, didn't I?"

Smith's wife nodded and said, "Yes, dear."

Holland tapped his fork against his dinner plate angrily.

"General Russell is in the process of having the whole manual for amphibious warfare rewritten. But, we still don't have any suitable landing craft to make a realistic attack on the fortified beaches those plans require. Everyone in the Navy knows there's a strong possibility of war with Japan, and they know . . . *they know . . . THEY KNOW* if that happens we're going to make frontal assaults on many fortified Japanese islands across the Pacific. The assholes in Washington *know* that and they *still* won't allocate funds for us. They won't listen when we tell them what we need to stage opposed landings. Damn it, it's Marines going across those beaches and spilling their blood. We've *got* to have more say!"

Ada looked at her husband disapprovingly. "Language, Holland. Please calm down, dear. It isn't good for you to get upset and angry while you're eating."

Smith looked at his wife and nodded. She was one of the few humans capable of calming him quickly. "I think of those men, those young men, not much older than our Victor, that are going to be killed on those beaches. I don't want one man, not one Marine, to die that doesn't have to. I've seen what can happen in France. I know how bad it will be. And we're asking these men, our Marines, to execute the toughest, most deadly military maneuver there is when we attack those fortified beaches. We have to give them the best chance of survival possible."

Ada nodded, "The Navy should certainly do that. Do you want more pot roast?"

"Yes." He shook his head and resumed his lecture, "The Pacific war is going to be completely different than anything we've done before. We need to increase our level of training now. Our equipment isn't adequate, and those landing craft—we've got to get good landing craft."

"If you get that boat from . . . from . . ."

"Higgins."

"Yes. That's the one. Will that solve all your problems?"

"No, not completely. The troops need to be landed in an amphibious vehicle until the major resistance is cleared from the beach. Something that will carry them up to an area where there's some defilade. Up to a point where . . ."

His wife rose from the dinner table and said, "I'll be right back with the roast." Ada started for the kitchen, but stopped abruptly, facing him. "Holland, they'll eventually see that you're right. You most always are. I'm sure you practically wrote the manual you were talking about. And besides, I know how strong-willed you are." A twinkle appeared in her eyes. "You'll nag them, push them and scream at them if you have to, right, Holland?"

Smith nodded, "I just hope they don't listen too late."

"You're sure we're actually going to war with the Japanese? The ones we've met at events in Washington all seem so well mannered, like the Amish back home in Pennsylvania."

Holland took a deep breath, "It isn't a question of whether we're going to fight them or not, the only question is when."

Ada said, "Oh," and walked away. As she passed the archway leading to the living room, she looked in and saw their son busily working on his homework. She said to herself very softly, "Holland, I certainly hope you're wrong."

7

Birth Pains
1935, Don Roebling
Clearwater, Florida

"Shit!" the mechanic snarled. The odd looking vessel gradually glided to a stop; little wavelets faded with the hopes of three men inside the floating metal monster. Its engine continued to run, but all motion had ceased. The man who had cursed shook his head and his shoulders drooped.

Don Roebling said, "Warren, try disengaging it and dropping it back in."

The mechanic grabbed two levers, pulling back on one then the other. "Here goes," he said as he engaged the gearbox and released the clutch. There was a whirring sound and metallic clicking, but the vessel remained immobile. Warren Cottrell repeated, "Shit!'

"It doesn't look like we have any choice; we have to put a heavier duty clutch in it." The third man pointed to a metal box mounted on the vehicle's side and floor. "That whole area is going to have to be reworked. Neither the Borg, nor the Allison will come close to fitting in there. The engine's mounts will have to change, plus who knows what else."

Roebling nodded, "No doubt you're right, Earl." Don scanned the dejected look on Earl De Bolt's face. "Don't be upset, buddy. You told me it probably wouldn't work. It was my decision to try that dampening device." Roebling turned around and motioned to a man in a twenty-eight foot cabin cruiser drifting a hundred yards behind. The boat's inboard came to life with a throaty rumble and slowly came to the rescue. As the cruiser passed by the vehicle, the man inside the boat called out, "The clutch again?"

"Yes," Roebling answered. "Let's get her back to shore."

The man in the cruiser, S.A. Williams, grunted, "Yep," and maneuvered the boat to tow the contraption that looked like a military tank with its top cut off. Three-quarters of the vehicle was submerged in the water. The ease with which he positioned the boat and assisted the men aboard in getting the steel tow ropes attached was proof that the procedure was an often repeated one. They were in motion toward the Clearwater Bay shoreline and Roebling's beautiful mansion in minutes.

"Well, at least, we don't have far to go this time," Warren said.

Roebling nodded his head as he gazed at his bay front home, 'Spottis Woods.' The estate, named for his wife, Florence Spottiswood Parker, occupied seven acres on the beautiful bay and was considered one of the finest on Florida's Gulf Coast. Don's machine shop was located on part of the property and was the place he and his crew of technicians were giving slow and painful birth to the amphibious rescue vehicle that demanded his time day and night. Roebling had christened his invention the "Alligator." The challenge, one much more difficult than he'd dreamed, consumed him.

"Don, it looks like your wife is getting ready for some kind of doings in the yard," Earl said. "You got guests starting to arrive."

Roebling checked his watch then peered at the formally dressed men and women strolling in his rear yard among the shrubs, white tables and chairs scattered on the lawn. He frowned. "Florence is having some of her friends over from her women's club. I was supposed to be there an hour ago."

Warren grinned, "She's going to be pissed at you, *again.*"

"She stays that way. Isn't that what wives are supposed to do?" Roebling looked down at his dirty tee shirt and grease-smeared coveralls. His huge bulk, housed beneath the cloth, produced copious quantities of perspiration, dampening the material in embarrassing locations. "I imagine when I go over to greet her friends, she'll be more upset."

"You going like that?" Warren asked.

"As soon as you fellows help me out of here, I'm going to stroll right over and join them."

"Uuuu-eeee, are you trying to get her furious at you? She damn near sent you packing when you put a dead rattlesnake under that serving dish for the Halloween party you had last fall," Earl said.

"Earl, you should have seen her the time he gave everybody at one of those high toned dinner parties those chocolates with the tobacco in the center." Warren chuckled. "It's a good thing she didn't have a gun right then."

The cabin cruiser's driver cut power as it neared a dock and ramp built at the waters edge. The boat veered away allowing the "Alligator" to drift to the point where its tracks ground into the sand. When functioning, those tracks provided locomotion for the amphibian.

"Don, you want me to tow it out or try to fix the clutch enough to get it up to the shop under its own power?" Cottrell hoisted himself onto the side of the Alligator.

"What will be easiest, Warren?"

"I have all the repair parts I need up there. It will be easier to repair the clutch and then nurse it back up to the shop."

"Okay, do that. Getting it up on the flat bed without the tracks working is a big problem, anyway."

Warren and Earl looked relieved and nodded their approval. Winching, towing, and maneuvering the twenty-four foot long, 14,350 pound vehicle wasn't easy. Earl pointed over Don's shoulder toward the house. "I think your wife wants to talk to you."

Roebling turned and recognized his wife's form approaching them. Florence's posture and features told Don her stroll wasn't a happy one. He called out to the man in the cruiser. "S.A., bring the boat over here and help me out. I think the sheriff," he pointed to his wife, "is looking to escort me to a lynching."

All the men laughed. The expression on Florence's face went from displeased to thunder-cloud.

* * *

Donald Roebling looked like a five year old child caught performing an evil prank. The shame and regret on his face were real, as they always were—after the fact.

Florence stood looking up at him. Her words were controlled and measured, not hostile. Don wished she'd shout and scream, for her self-control left him nothing to justify an angry, defensive response. She continued, "You must have known how I would feel. Those are *my* friends. Don't you see how it embarrassed me? Don, people know you're different and they accept that. But they also know you're not showing any respect for me when you do something like you did today. I didn't appreciate your actions or your crude jokes."

"I'm sorry, dear."

"I don't doubt that you are. Don't you see I need something from our relationship, too?"

"Florence, I try to see that you have everything you want."

Don's wife put her hands on his shoulders. "You are one of the most generous people I've ever met—with your money and with anything you own. What you aren't generous with is your time. At least, Don, not with me. You spend more time with your hobbies than we share together. Do you see how it makes me feel, knowing that you'd rather spend hours looking at your stamp collection than at me? You talk to your buddies on the HAM radio system more than we do. I understand the passion you and your father have for the development of the hurricane rescue vehicle, it's truly important. Don't you understand I need some of that passion? I want children."

"Let's not discuss that again. You know..."

Florence saw the hurt in her husband's face and interrupted him. "Don, Don, Don, I'm not going to lecture you on losing weight, or even cutting down on eating candy, ice cream and cookies. I've done that enough to know that it doesn't do any good. Just please consider it, if not for me, for your own health."

Roebling's vision dropped to the floor. "I promise I will."

"I sincerely hope you will, Don." Florence left unspoken the words, *or something must change.*

* * *

"We *are* making steady progress, Dad. It just seems each time we take two steps forward in one area we're forced to take a step back in another. I had the Coast Guard and the Red Cross look at the Alligator, neither was interested enough to buy one. They like the concept and agree they need a rescue vehicle, but don't think it's ready, yet."

John Roebling took a puff on his cigar and leaned back in his comfortable chair. He looked through the window of Red Hill, his Lake Placid home. His thoughts ran back three years ago when he and his son, Donald, had sat in the same room and agreed to pursue the project. He was pleased that Don was truly devoted to the amphibian's development and was focused on its completion. Both the machine and his son were showing improvement; John just wished the progress was a little faster. "I don't suppose that the Alligator will be ready for this year's hurricane season, will it?"

"Will we have a unit that functions? Yes. Will it be what is really needed? No." Don's expression left no doubt as to his statement's finality.

John nodded. "I'm happy to hear we're that far. I'm going to visit Clearwater in a few weeks to see it. I know I'll be pleased. Everything you've done previously hasn't disappointed me." What really *pleased* John Roebling was the look of pride on his son's face. "Can you give me a thumb nail report on the current problems?"

Don proceeded with enthusiasm. "Dad, it all goes back to the two major rules I established when I started to design the Alligator. First, we have to keep the vehicle light enough to keep it buoyant in adverse wind and water conditions, yet sturdy enough for rugged land use. Second, the propulsion systems for land and water can't be bulky and cumbersome and take so much space that the vehicle is useless to perform its task." Don paused and rubbed his hands together. "It's the approaches and innovations we've used to solve those problems that are creating our new ones."

"Normally, true progress doesn't come quickly, easily, cheaply, or without set-backs. That's to be expected," the elder Roebling said.

Don Roebling nodded. "You know that we're using aluminum to lighten the vehicle. Doing that has greatly reduced the vehicle's weight and has accomplished what we wanted in respect to the Alligator's buoyancy and has allowed us to increase its payload. The problem we're finding is that we have to develop a whole new technology to work with aluminum's softness. No one has used the material in the way we are, so methods used in cutting and shaping aren't common knowledge. We've found wood cutting tools and techniques work better than those used for steel. And welding, riveting, or joining it create very different problems. For example, Warren had to come up with a new rivet design to keep our work from falling apart. Without the innovations we've developed—well, you know the first model we built literally broke in two after a few miles over rough terrain. We have most of those problems solved, but we know some aren't, *and* I'm sure more we haven't anticipated will arise."

"You're solving them—that's the most important issue," John told his son. "It's like the propulsion system you've come up with. Using a track system for both land and water propulsion. Pure genius!"

"That's another good example, Dad. I'm sure what we're doing will work, eventually. The speed we're able to generate in the water is disappointing. And the marine maneuverability needs to be improved. Our best speed so far is 2.3 mph. The paddles we've installed on the tracks make the drive assembly fragile. It's difficult to operate the Alligator for three miles on hard ground without a breakdown. If we increase the size of the paddle surface area to increase our water speed, the breaking problem is compounded."

"How have you increased the size of the paddle?"

"We increased the depth by a half-inch—that gave us 1.4 mph more speed in water. That got us to 3.7 mph. Like I said, it made the system even more fragile on ground. We hardly traveled a mile before the assembly broke."

John thought for several seconds. "What about lengthening the paddle instead of increasing the depth? That will give you more surface area. Your tread is eight inches wide, correct?"

"Yes."

"If you extended the length out an inch to each side, you would get the same amount of surface area addition as deepening the paddle a half-inch. Why not try that?"

"Hmmm." Don averted his eyes to the ceiling, visualizing the mechanism. He spoke as he thought. "That should give us the increase in speed alright. They might catch on things outside the treads...maybe extending two inches inside would—no I don't like that."

"Do you have a blueprint of the track assembly to work from?" John raised his eyebrow over one eye as he spoke. He felt he already knew the answer.

"No. You know my philosophy on that. It takes more time, expense and effort to draw everything up while the design is so fluid. Take what happened two days ago. We made some changes to increase the tread assembly's strength as an experiment. It resulted in making the clutch we'd been using too light duty to do the job. We'll have to change the motor mounts, the engine and the transmission connections, and install a new clutch. Even the size of the cover will change. Earl and Warren will have everything made tomorrow. We'd still be making drawings a week from now if we did our development that way. I want to spend our time concentrating on making the Alligator simple and rugged. Once we get a finished design, I'll get blueprints made." Don looked out the window. "I can visualize how the track assembly would look if the tracks were…" He stopped and looked back at his father. Don Roebling smiled and slapped his hands down on his huge thighs. "I think I know the answer to more water speed *and* land reliability."

8

A Warning to a "Mad" Genius
1935, Holland Smith
General Russell's Headquarters,
Washington, DC

"Have a seat, Holland." General Russell stood to greet his guest as they exchanged salutes. General Russell, a dark haired, strongly built man with intense eyes smiled at what he considered one of his best officers.

"It's good to see you again, General." Smith returned the smile as both men seated themselves at a small conference table. Russell had a small stack of file folders piled in front of him and Holland Smith carried a briefcase.

"How was your trip from San Francisco?" Russell asked.

"Pleasant and uneventful. I brought Ada with me. She wanted to visit some friends and family. Since my new appointment, we haven't had a lot of time to talk. The train trip allowed me to catch up on what's going on in my family and to acquaint Ada with what my new job entails." Smith removed some papers from his briefcase and placed them on the table.

"Good. I'll call the wife and see if we can have dinner

while you're here." The general picked up a file and waved it in the air. "Holland, I believe you're going to be the best Chief of Staff for the Department of the Pacific that's ever held the position. Your passion for developing our amphibious capabilities will make it so. So . . . let's get right to it. I want to talk about your readiness assessment letters and I want your opinion on what Japanese intentions are in the Central and South Pacific areas." The general put the folder down and removed a multi-page letter from it. "To begin, I agree whole-heartedly with most of what you've said. There is no doubt we need the increase in training you've called for. We certainly need the additional updated equipment. And, I agree that the core items are better boats to land our troops and equipment. But, before we start into our discussions, I'd like to give you a piece of personal advice." General Russell paused, prompting Smith to speak.

"Please, sir, I'd be appreciative of anything you'd have to say."

"You may feel differently after I've finished." Russell cocked his head to one side and stared intently into Holland's eyes. "I want to tell you a story. You're from the rural South, you'll understand." The General leaned back. "There was this old hound dog that was very protective of his owner's watermelon fields. Those watermelons were the best in the county and a lot of unsavory folks wanted to steal them. But that didn't bother the old hound. That dog would get in the middle of the farm road going to the melon field and stop anybody that tried to steal them. He had the right intentions and he was doing what was best for the farmer. One day a car with the word 'Sheriff' written on the side pulled in the road. Of course, that didn't bother old bow-wow; he stood in the middle of the road anyway. Guess what? That car didn't stop. It squashed that good, faithful hound and the farmer lost one of his best and most valuable friends. You see, what that old dog didn't realize is that sometimes people in high places don't care what's right or about the folks that are defending it." The General leaned forward. His features were stony and serious, his eyes flashing. "Holland, the stuff you've been writing in these memos is correct. But, some of the things you're saying don't help the Corps or you. Your comments about the Navy upper echelons are true. Certainly the points you've made about the use of funds hit home. So are some of your observations about inter-service relations. But, Holland, plain and simple—you're poking a hornet's nest. You have to know how far back to stand, *and* when to quit. Understand?"

"Yes sir." Smith looked taken aback by his idol's comments.

"Don't change *what* you're saying. Change *how* you're saying it. Be diplomatic. Talk more about the situations than the people involved. Look, I'd never have gotten the

Fleet Marine Force approved or gotten the Officer Selection Act through without the cooperation of the same people whose toes you've been stomping. We're not going to get the equipment we need, money to train and the freedom to do what needs to be done by alienating the Navy's command structure and personnel from the Joint Chiefs of Staff's offices. I know talking around the issues will stick in your craw; it sure sticks in mine. Calling a son-of-a-bitch, a son-of-a-bitch, might make you feel better, and honest, and right, but it isn't getting authorizations approved. Remember, *we are part of the Navy*, and it's a political world out there."

"I'll keep that firmly in mind, General." Smith realized John Russell was giving him good advice. He hoped he'd be disciplined enough to follow it.

"Good. We can't afford to have good men like you end up commanding the latrines in Louisiana." General Russell looked at the letter in front of him. "You're convinced that we're going to be in a conflict with Japan in the next five to ten years. I agree. With what's happening in China, and with our efforts to help the Chinese, I'm sure we'll eventually cause the Japs to either back off or to fight us. They need the resources. The state department is threatening oil embargoes and restricting what they can buy from us. They won't stand for that. The militarists control their government. My bet is we'll be fighting them."

"I think it's inevitable. We've known since Pete Ellis did his intelligence and planning that the Japanese are planning for war with us. We were together in France and talked about it. He said when Teddy Roosevelt sided with the Russians at the end of their war, some hot heads on the Imperial General Staff claimed we caused them to lose face and wanted to fight us then. After the way they licked the Russians, they think they can whip anyone. They've had their way in China. Our efforts to keep them out of Indochina and the Indies are just going to add to the tension. The big question I have is, how will it start?"

Russell put his hand to his chin and pursed his lips. "Do you know the Orange plan is still the basis to update our plans? When Ellis devised the Orange plan he assumed the Japs would come directly after us. Not Australia. Not the Indies. Not Hong Kong, or Singapore. That means they'll probably hit our fringe bases. Guam. Wake Island. Maybe even the Philippines. Those are all inside the perimeter the mandated islands give them. It makes sense, too. The British and the US combined keep them reined in. If either of us were out of the picture, I think they believe they'd have a free hand in all of Southeast Asia."

"Pete Ellis thought that. His guess was they thought they'd make out better fighting us than the British Navy. He theorized since we'd be their enemy of choice; they might even try to invade the west coast, taking Hawaii along the way. If you're asking if I believe Ellis' Orange plan is still valid today, my answer is yes. If we go across the Central Pacific like he called for and seize dozens of small islands, we've got to do the amphibious tactical revamping we have here," Holland patted his brief case, "quickly. The problem is getting larger weekly. Many more atolls have been fortified since Pete gathered intelligence on those bases in 1923."

"Pete was one of the sharpest strategists we've ever had in the Corps. He sure had the Japanese strategy figured. We'll never know what happened to him on Palau. You know the Jap officials claimed he died of acute alcohol poisoning. I imagine the poisoning part is correct enough." The General shook his head. "It's amazing how closely he predicted what is going on in the Pacific today. He seemed to know precisely how things would proceed."

"Pete and I used to talk about concerns he had about how things ended in Europe and what was likely to happen in the Pacific. He said we'd be back in Europe in fifteen years and I disagreed. I thought he was crazy, but now, I don't know. Hitler's changed everything over there. Ellis thought Japan was the next war, however. Pete believed the Jap leaders had too many ambitions and too little space. He said the Japanese wouldn't have enough resources to fight a long war against the British or us. Their war plan would have to be to keep it short and shock us into a quick peace when either the Brits or us were distracted somewhere else." Smith took a deep breath. "We both agreed if a war broke out with Japan, it would be a tough one. They have a large, well trained Army that's fanatical. Even with the new aircraft carriers we're building we have to get within 300 miles to attack. In order to defeat them, we've got to cross 3700 miles of ocean, create bases and defend them. The only way we saw to do it then and the way I still see it now, is one frontal assault . . . one landing after another." Smith stopped talking long enough to remove an inch thick bound document from his briefcase. "We're going to need this. I reviewed the draft for the *Landing Operations Manual.* It looks very good. I made notes and suggestions as you requested."

Russell smiled, "A lot of it should have been familiar. Over half the ideas in that manual were drafted straight from your letters, exercise plans and suggestions. I think Walt Ansel did a great job gathering your ideas and others and putting the manual together. He gathered his information from the best minds in the Corps." The General thumbed through his file folders until he reached the one he wanted. "Have you seen any of these pictures?" He handed Smith a thick file folder. "These are combat photos of fighting between the Chinese and the Japanese. They were made during Jap actions when they invaded and occupied more of the Chinese mainland. You probably have seen some of them, but take a look anyway. I want you to concentrate on some of their equipment and how they use it. The Japanese Army has developed its amphibious capabilities to a fine art."

Holland Smith silently took the folder from General Russell. He opened the file and whistled. A half-inch thick stack of photos, a pack of newspaper clippings and Marine documents were filled with images and descriptions of Japanese troops and materials. Weapons reports, photos of troops in full battle dress, casualties from both sides and pictures of the destruction of towns, industries and farms told the full story. Ample evidence of the Imperial Army's brutality existed in photos showing many beheaded Chinese soldiers, bayoneted children and mutilated women. However, Smith concentrated the most on the photos of Japanese troops engaged in amphibious landings. He pulled pictures of Japanese landing craft from the stack as he reviewed them. When Holland finished he asked, "Where did these come from?"

"The Chinese, Japanese newspapers, mercenaries, freelance photographers, but the best came from the Swedish embassy and economic mission people. The Swedes got most of those photos by paying off a German military attaché." Russell sighed and shrugged his shoulders. "The Swedes are like the Swiss, they both disapprove and want no part of war, but they don't mind working with both sides and profiting from it."

Holland glanced up from the pictures. "The Germans are getting much friendlier with the Japanese. That's a strange combination, particularly since the Japs ended up getting almost all of Germany's Pacific holdings mandated to them after the War."

"Yes, they're forming a closer alliance. It's accelerated, after Hitler became chancellor in '33. Mussolini and Hitler are peas out of the same pod. That moves the balance of power in Europe their way. It's very obvious why they've teamed up. The more aggression Japan perpetrates in the Far East, the more we're distracted from what's going on in Europe. And the reverse. Hitler's tearing up or ignoring all the Versailles agreements. We aren't stopping him. The British aren't. The French are screaming, but doing nothing. Russia and England are at each others throats. Japan and Russia don't trust each other. The British, French and us are like cats trying to watch three mouse holes at the same time, not knowing which the enemy will appear from next. The only problem is there are poisonous snakes in those holes, not mice. As far as the Germans are concerned, they get a bonus. As long as Japan threatens the Russians, it keeps Stalin and the Soviets from being as aggressive in Eastern Europe as they might be otherwise. The Russians remember the beating they took the last time they fought the Japs. I think that's why the Soviets are aiding the Chinese so heavily. Besides trying to get communism established in parts of China, they create a buffer between themselves and Japan."

"All that makes sense." Smith's attention returned to the pictures. He selected four photos and placed them in front of General Russell. "Look at these. They sure illustrate Japanese amphibious techniques. They know the critical objective required to make a successful landing is getting their troops ashore with the smallest loss possible. They're very careful about where they land and they have the proper equipment to stage an amphibious operation. Their strategy calls for avoiding a frontal assault at the initial landing point. Stealth and surprise is their first priority." Smith pointed at the photos. "Notice every one of these is at a location where there is minimal space between the landing craft and cover for their soldiers after they leave the boat. That's the key, General, shorten the *time* men are exposed to fire from the point they leave the landing craft until they reach cover and can start to fight. Look at their boats. They can get very close to the shoreline and let the troops run for defilade." Smith pointed to one of the photos. "See that. See the bow—my guess is they're developing some type of craft that will allow them to drop a ramp as they hit shore and run right off." Smith shook his head. "With the motor launches or whale boats we'd have to use now, we'd get our boys slaughtered if we landed on a fortified beach."

"A lot of the Army personnel I've talked to say amphibious operations of any kind are disasters waiting to happen." Russell leaned back in his chair. "Re-convince me that it's not."

"It's not if you can follow the Japanese formula, use equipment similar to theirs, and use the tactics I've proposed to cope with the type places we'll have to invade. Unfortunately, many landings we'll have to make will be frontal assaults. That will make them more costly. Where the Japs are fighting in China, they have the luxury of lots of places to land. The Chinese have huge manpower reserves, but crude weaponry. China's a big place with plenty of waterways. It's impossible for the Chinese to defend everyplace you can land troops. The Japanese simply avoid fortified landing spots, choose one that's not, and maneuver around a flank. We won't have that working for us. We can use the type boats they do. Hopefully, we can improve on them. A boat I'm trying to get approved for testing is similar. You've seen my letters on the Eureka, the boat Andrew Higgins is building. But, even that might not be enough. Most of our target islands are very small with a very limited number of landing beaches. Many have coral reefs surrounding them. There's no room for maneuver. We can't surprise the Japs the way they surprise the Chinese. Aerial reconnaissance should allow them to spot our invasion convoys days in advance."

Smith took a paper and pencil from his briefcase. He drew a circle on it to represent an island. In the circle, he scratched a large number of X's. "Those X's represent fixed fortifications the Jap defenders will rely on. We have to eliminate as many as possible with naval gunfire," he scribbled over some, "and with aerial bombardment," Smith scratched through more, "but, it will be impossible to eliminate them all." Holland tapped the pencil point on the X's representing the island's remaining defenses. "Our naval fire and aerial bombardment has to continue until right before our men set foot on the beach to keep the defenders pinned down and make their fire ineffective." Holland stared intensely into General Russell's eyes. "Then it's most important that we attack immediately and continuously. The traditional army tactic of accumulating your force and reorganizing puts the whole landing in danger. If you do that, the soldiers on the landing beach become sitting ducks that artillery and automatic weapons can pulverize. We must attack as soon as we're ashore, get our troops off the beach as rapidly as possible, reduce the fortifications, and continue moving even if we have to by-pass strong-points and clean them up later. Isolating their positions makes it easier for us to deal with the enemy in pockets and makes it difficult for them to organize an effective counter attack."

"That takes the tremendous coordination between the Corps and the Navy you're recommending. I understand why you're pressing so hard for extensive training for pre-assault bombardment, rapid deployment and quick penetration off the beach. The logistics to support that kind of an operation are staggering, new technology is going to be required." General Russell returned Smith's intense stare. "Holland, let's assume that we can overcome the logistics, train our troops to function the way we want them *and* that the Navy will give us the support and coordination we need to make a series of amphibious assaults successful. What is the single greatest concern you have in using the tactics you've outlined?"

Smith didn't hesitate a second. "The landing craft. We don't have anything that will allow us to get from the transports to the beach without exposing our men to murderous fire for too long a period of time."

"And you think Higgins' boat design, the Eureka, will solve that problem?"

Smith paused before he answered. "If the boat tests well and if we can find a way to fit the boat with a ramp, it will put us on an equal footing with the Japanese. That's just equal. If we can select beaches we can get the boats up to, it gives our tactics a chance of success." Smith hesitated again, pursed his lips, and said, "To answer you honestly . . . no. There are situations where no boat will do what's needed. A lot of Pacific Islands have cliffs with limited numbers of landing beaches. The Japanese will concentrate on those. I'm sure the defenders will clear off much of the cover to improve their field of fire. Every square foot will have weapons aiming at it. And, like I said, most are surrounded with coral reefs and bars that no boat could pass over. The passes through the reefs are sure to have artillery and mortars zeroed in on them. Going through those narrow gaps would be suicidal. I'm sure the Japs will put anti-boat devices and barbwire on the beaches. We need something that can roll right over the reefs, maneuver through obstructions, crash through barbwire and carry the men across the open area on the beach right up to cover."

"That's a tall order, Holland."

"Yes, it is. But General Russell, anything that will save Marine lives, we've got to have."

* * *

9

Testing . . . 1,2,3, Crossing T's and Dotting I's
1936, Don Roebling
Panther Marsh, West Central Florida

The mosquitoes buzzed over the grassy waters, their wings creating a low pitched symphony to serenade and warn the marsh creatures of their presence. A water moccasin wound its way through green stems and leaves, looking for frogs or whatever else nature was serving for breakfast in the tepid air the sun's morning rays had just invaded. Competition for the day's first meal appeared. A Great Blue Heron touched down in the foot deep water a few yards distant from the snake. The bird eyed the snake, but it was far too large for the heron to consider it as a viable meal. The marsh was a peaceful quiet setting where nature's dramas played out each day far away from the prying eyes and interference of humans.

From some bushes that marked the shore, a deer cautiously eased through the branches for a morning drink and to nibble on the tender grass. The doe was alert to all the many dangers the swamp hid. She avoided the snake and eyed the Heron suspiciously before lowering her head to take a drink. Her head bobbed up nervously, looking for some threat she'd missed in her first vigil. The deer turned its head in every direction, allowing its soft brown eyes to carefully examine its surroundings while its keen nose sampled the air. After a full minute, the doe decided it was safe to have its morning "coffee" and resume trimming the marsh grass. The animals head and tongue dropped to water level.

The deer was the first to sense an invader. Her sensitive ears twitched before the other creatures had any warning that the marsh's peaceful routine was being shattered. She raised her head and looked in the direction of a faint rumbling noise. The sound originated from beyond a stand of cypress trees that hid whatever was creating the bedlam. The doe's legs tensed. She prepared to take flight if the strange intruding sounds were generated by something dangerous. The sound of an engine soon became identifiable.

A large white object appeared from behind the cypress trees. Behind it trailed a spray of mud-tinged water as it moved surprisingly fast through the mucky marsh. The vehicle crunched toward the deer. The doe had seen enough. She bolted long before the tracks that propelled the vehicle were visible or the airboat trailing the "Alligator" came into view. The heron took wing within seconds of the deer's departure. The bird squawked, protesting the invasion of its secluded home. Only the moccasin ignored the rumble and vibration created by the amphibious tractor as the vehicle raced through the marsh.

Five people's heads were sticking up above the rescue craft's front and sides as it moved through the mud and grass clogged water. Don Roebling, his father John,, and Don's three technicians bounced around as the vehicle rolled over a submerged log.

"All right!" Warren yelled. The Alligator had weathered another severe test of its durability. "We were doing a minimum of 12 mph when we ran over the log."

Earl De Bolt patted the machine's side and said, "Good old girl."

"Impressive, very impressive!" John Roebling slapped his son on the back.

"We've come a long way, but I still have some areas to improve before we have a final product." Don Roebling directed his next words to Cottrell. "Let's take it for a swim, Warren."

"Okay boss." Cottrell pulled some levers and the Alligator abruptly changed direction.

S.A. Williams pointed to grass on one side of the tractor. "Look at the size of that water moccasin!" The snake slithered out of the way. "It's got to be a five footer."

Warren purposely guided the vehicle at a copse of scrubby bushes that marked the edge of a hidden marsh pond. It would provide another test for the tractor. Warren mumbled, "Here we go," as he crashed the machine into and through the willows. The Alligator responded by mangling the tree-lets in its path, leaving an eight foot wide breach in the green wall. The tractor lurched down at an angle as it entered the pond.

Water boiled behind the tracks as the pond deepened enough for the Alligator to become a barge. Don Roebling grabbed his father's shoulder with one hand. "Dad, this is one of the areas that still needs improvement. I want to get more speed here. We've doubled it from our first model. She'll do a little over 5 mph in water and we're still getting a respectable 18 mph on dry land."

"Is that the final improvement you want to make, son?" John asked.

"No. I've got several problems left to solve. Some are minor. One is a major glitch." Don Roebling shook his head. "I haven't figured out what I want to do about it."

"I'm sorry, I couldn't hear you." John raised his voice to be heard over the engine's roar.

Don waved a hand back and forth like a flag. "Let's talk when we get back to the shed so we don't have to shout."

John nodded.

"Hey, Warren, take us back to the nest," Don said.

The amphibian rescue vehicle crossed the little pond in a few minutes preparatory to its crawling out on the shoreline. Warren aimed the machine at a pole barn built on the property next to the lake. The Roebling's had built the shed to shelter and work on their invention at the test site. The Alligator emerged from the water and moved across the bank effortlessly. The driver stopped the machine next to a small crane that was used to handle materials when maintaining the Alligator and for getting Donald Roebling's bulky body in and out of the vehicle. A swinging seat hung from its cable.

After all the occupants exited the Alligator, Don and his father circled the vehicle. Don stopped at its front. "I believe we're very close to having a practical, efficient rescue amphibian, but—there always seems to be a *but.*" He pointed to the track assembly. "There's still the biggest problem we have. The tracks won't hold up long when we operate the Alligator on hard land. The harder the surface, the quicker we have a breakdown. We seldom can go more than a couple of miles over really solid ground, like pavement. I've done all I can think of to strengthen the tread chain. Angling the paddles on a diagonal has helped durability a little. You've seen the improvement the model III provides in its speed and maneuverability in water. We are so close! The unit is 2550 pounds lighter than the original. When we try to climb the unit out of a canal or river it wants to hang up if the incline is very steep, but I believe I know how to solve that problem. I know how to lighten the unit more and improve its performance. Starting next week we're going to tear the prototype down and build the Model IV. I think it will be a great unit—lighter, faster, with room for rescuing forty people. The only thing I'm concerned about is the track assembly. The calculations I've made show the chain and components should be plenty strong. I don't understand why we're having such a big problem."

John Roebling knelt down and examined the track assembly. After looking at it from several angles, he looked up at his son. "It certainly looks *more* than strong enough. I can't see any obvious design flaws in the tracks or assembly." He hesitated for a few seconds. "Don, have you thought about changing the mounting or suspension systems? There might be something in one of those designs that's stressing the chain so impossibly that no track assembly you'd manufacturer could be made strong enough."

"That's interesting." Don turned and called to Warren Cottrell. "Hey, Warren, come over here for a moment."

Warren put down a grease gun with which he was lubricating the suspension idler wheels. He smiled as he approached and said, "Whatcha need boss?"

"Remember about four weeks ago when we tried climbing the canal bank and had trouble when the angle got steeper than twenty-two degrees? Then the same day, when we ran the vehicle up and down the road testing the latest track modification, it snapped for seemingly no reason?"

"Yep."

"Remember talking about things we could do to make it climb the bank easier *and* possibly reduce the strain on the track assembly? We had several ideas of ways to change the suspension."

"Sure do."

"Well, we're going to make them. I want to go with a totally new suspension system. I want to do away with the bogie wheels and install roller bearings right in the chain track like I discussed. And I want to go to fixed idler blocks like you and Earl suggested instead of the idler wheels like we're using now. It may solve our breakage problem and I'm sure it will give us a smoother performance on steep inclines. We'll add the curved, cupped cleats to the tracks at the same time."

"Now you're talkin', boss." Cottrell removed a cigarette from his pocket and lit it. "When do you want to start?"

"This afternoon."

Warren said, "Hallelujah." As he walked away he yelled, "Hey, Earl and S.A., forget that fishing trip this afternoon, we're going to start the Model IV!"

Don smiled, nodded to his father and said, "Dad, I believe the Alligator will be ready for hurricane rescues by the '37 season. We'll be ready to save lives. I'll be able to give something back to this country, just like you've always told me I should."

John Roebling smiled. Maybe Don did listen once-in-a-while. What John didn't say was the new Hoover Dike being built around Lake Okeechobee would eliminate the original reason for the vehicle's construction. True, there were other areas were the vehicle could be used to rescue. And John Roebling didn't want to do anything that would interfere with Don's devotion to the project. It had grounded the boy, if not solving all his son's short-comings.

* * *

"Do you think there is any chance of you two reaching a reconciliation?" John Roebling's worried expression showed his concern.

Don Roebling shook his head. "No. She wants me to change more than I can or want to, Dad. She says I march to the beat of my own drummer. She knew that before we married. I'm heavy, yes. But, I don't weigh much more than when we were dating."

"Your mother spoke to Florence and there are some legitimate issues. Your weight isn't the big thing." John leaned forward in his chair. "Don, you have to be objective when you look at yourself. She said you're constantly embarrassing her by pulling wild pranks on her friends."

"Her friends lack a sense of humor."

"Borrowing a corpse from the local funeral home and having it sitting at the dinner table during one of Florence's party is not funny!" John said.

"I was just sending them a message: they're all stiffs." Don shrugged his shoulders. "That might have been out of line, but they're a bunch of self-impressed assholes."

John shook his head in disgust. "They're still her friends. She said you wouldn't take her places she wants to go."

"I never kept her from going anywhere she wanted, or from doing anything she wanted to do. I've gone with her when I could do so physically and not feel out of place."

"Did you promise her to try to lose weight, but never did it?"

Don looked at his father defiantly. "I tried."

John shook his head. "Son, she said you constantly give away gifts that are exorbitant for no legitimate reason."

Don scowled, "I'm generous. The Boy Scouts needed a building, so I built them one. If a civic organization needs money, I give some."

"Florence said you gave away your airplane to someone simply because he told you he liked it."

Don looked out the window of his Clearwater mansion. "That didn't hurt her."

"She wanted children—"

"I told her we could adopt."

"Don, she wanted her own."

Don Roebling struggled from his chair and said, "I don't want to talk about this anymore," and left the room. His father sighed deeply and stood up. He'd have lots of time on the long trip from Clearwater to Lake Placid to determine how he would tell his wife, Margaret, he saw no hope for his son's marriage to Florence. It was troubling. He believed Florence was a fine woman and losing her would be Donald's loss; a very major loss. Knowing his son was stubborn, eccentric and hopelessly spoiled made John feel guilty. Knowing that the boy was empathetic, hard-working and generous to those around him, particularly to those-in-need, offset some of the pain.

10

Obstacles, but Light at the End of the Tunnel
1937, Holland Smith
USMC Headquarters, Washington, DC

A corporal stood at Holland Smith's office door. Seemingly out of the blue, Smith had been promoted to the rank of full colonel and transferred to Washington under the command of Major General Thomas Holcomb. His first assignment was as Director of Operations and Training. He was now in a position to supervise the building of the modern amphibious force he'd been advocating for years. Part of that opportunity was to obtain the necessary equipment to make this new brand of warfare a success. The corporal tapped the door frame and cleared his throat to get Smith's attention.

Smith was so engrossed in the report he was reading he failed to hear the corporal's knock. The corporal said, "Colonel Smith, sir, I know you asked not to be disturbed, but there's a gentleman who would like to speak to you."

Holland frowned, but remained silent. He raised his eyebrows and lifted his hands, palms upward, prompting the corporal to continue.

"His name is Andrew Higgins. He's here about some

form of boat he claims you're familiar with."

Smith's frown quickly disappeared and was replaced by a smile. "Oh, I don't mind being interrupted by Higgins anytime. Send him in, corporal."

Holland heard voices outside his office. Andrew Higgins walked through his office door, saying, "Congratulations, *Colonel* Smith."

"Thank you. In time we'll find out whether I deserve it or not. Andrew, it's good to see you again." Smith stood and welcomed his guest warmly, displaying his inner feelings, an unusual act for someone who avoided displays of affection. Holland motioned to a chair next to his desk. "Have a seat." As Higgins eased downward, Smith asked, "What brings you all the way to Washington from New Orleans?"

"I'm giving it another try, Holland." Higgins smiled wryly. "Maybe there's some new faces in high places that will look at the Eureka more favorably." Higgins pointed to the placard sitting on Smith's desk. "Director of Operations and Planning, maybe he can help me."

"You know I will—and have been," Holland said. He rose from his chair and walked to a world map hanging on the wall. "It's damned important we get your boat, or one like it, soon. Japan has taken most of what they want in China." He ran his finger over the map from Hawaii to Borneo. "This is what I'm sure they'll go after next. Andy, we need your boat to fight the bastards out there. It's 98% ocean. We can't fight and win a war with what we have to stage landings today." Smith returned to his seat. "I wrote a letter to our friends at the Bureau of Ships asking them to purchase a prototype of one of your boats right before I was transferred here. I hope that helps you."

"Maybe it already has. You know, I've offered the Eureka to the Navy every year since 1927. Most years they've turned me down flat. No explanation. Nothing. This year they are allowing me to make a pitch, anyway." Higgins removed a blueprint and several pages of typed specifications from a briefcase. "These are copies of the plans for the latest version."

"Hmmm," Smith murmured as he spread the drawing on his desk. "I see you've changed the tunnel to protect the propellers even more. It's also a little shorter and a little wider. Why did you shorten it?"

"Holland, that's what the Navy insists on. They won't discuss a unit over thirty feet long. Do you know why that's so?"

"No, I don't."

"Well, I'm going into a meeting with them in a little less than an hour and I hope to find out." Andrew rubbed his chin. "Take a hard look at those specs and the drawing, Holland. Tell me if you see anything you'd like changed or improved."

Smith nodded and carefully examined the papers in front of him. He silently pointed to items on the drawing without making comment. After fifteen minutes of careful study, he said, "Andy, it looks good, but we need one to test before I can really answer you. The only thing I'd ask is if the boat could be built with heavier plating or if the bow and sides can be armored to reduce casualties."

"Yes, we could add a little. If the Navy would consider a craft around forty feet, I could do a lot more for you on that." Higgins stood up. "I've got to go get ready to visit the Bureau."

Smith started to fold and gather the documents, but Higgins stopped him. "Those are yours, Holland."

Holland looked very serious and said, "Thanks." As Andrew Higgins left the room, Smith added, "Stop by when you're done. I'd like to know how things went."

* * *

The corporal, grinning and suppressing a laugh, stood in Smith's office doorway. He said, "Colonel, I have a phone call for you. It's Andrew Higgins, sir."

"You look like you swallowed a feather. What's so funny?" Holland asked.

"Mr. Higgins has quite a sense of humor. I asked him how the meeting went. He said, *The meeting went okay, but it was like being in a maze with a bunch of blind rats with a cat chasing them. The only thing is, I couldn't figure out if I was the cat or one of the rats.*"

Smith chuckled. "Put him through."

In seconds, the phone rang. Holland picked up the handset, not being sure what to expect. He guessed that the fact Higgins hadn't returned in person was a bad omen, but Andrew's words to the corporal had been up-beat. "Hello, Andrew. I'm anxious to know if you were successful. How did *we* do?"

"I'll tell you tonight, if I can talk you into bringing your wife and meeting me for dinner for a small celebration." Higgins said.

"Damn, that sounds good! How ma—"

Higgins cut off Holland, "I'd prefer to cover that to-night. I'm still at the Bureau and I don't want to tie up one of their phones for a long period of time. Do you think you and Ada can make it tonight?"

"I'm sure we can."

"Alright, meet me at the Hilton at 7:30 if that's okay with you. If that's a problem you can call me there. I'm in room 238."

* * *

The maitre d' seated Ada and Holland Smith with Andrew Higgins as they exchanged greetings. The very up-scale restaurant, located in the hotel, featured a band playing Glenn Miller music and a dance floor.

"I love Glenn Miller's songs. Isn't that, *In the Mood?*" Ada asked. She watched the band leader swing his baton in a more symbolic than functional motion based on the bands playing.

"Yes, it sure is." Andrew Higgins wrinkled up his hose. "Not a very good imitation I'm afraid."

"Oh, they don't sound too bad," Ada said.

"You'll have to excuse my musical snobbishness. Being from New Orleans, we're used to the best when it comes to musicians." Higgins added, "But, I agree it's hard to beat anything Glenn Miller writes."

The maitre d' shifted from foot to foot impatiently, "May I see the lady and gentlemen have something to drink? I'll give your order to the waiter who'll be serving you."

"Is champagne okay for everyone?" Higgins asked.

"Wonderful," Ada said and Holland nodded.

Andrew spoke to the maitre d', asking him to pick a good selection and sent the man shuffling off. "I'm sure you want to know what happened over at the Bureau today, so I won't keep you in suspense any longer. It was a struggle, but we got the go ahead to build a prototype for testing."

"Great. How many?" Smith asked.

"One. And we were lucky to get it. In fact, if it hadn't been for Lieutenant Commander Goddard, I'm not sure we'd have gotten that. Do you remember Goddard, Holland?" Higgins asked.

"Yes. Good man. I'm glad to hear he got his promotion."

"He helped a lot. But, let me start at the beginning." Higgins leaned forward in his seat. "I don't think Commander Markham had approved meeting with me. I had the distinct feeling from what he said and how he acted at the meeting's beginning that he was seeing me out of courtesy. I'm guessing Goddard pushed someone on his staff to set up the audience and vouched for the Eureka's feasibility. Goddard has a new assignment and was there as an advisor because of his familiarity with prospective landing craft. Anyway, the first words out of Markham's mouth were negative. He said they'd spent all of the R & D budget for the year, but he'd look at what I'd brought with me. I spread the drawings out; he yawned and really didn't pay too much attention at first. However, the people on his staff did. As they kept saying they liked this or that, Markham finally got involved. We'd spent over an hour looking at the prints and exchanging information when one of his lieutenant JG's said he thought the Navy ought to be trying one." Higgins smirked and leaned back. "I could see Markham thinking about how he should proceed—whether he should authorize one because his whole staff was talking favorably about the Eureka, or turn us down as his bosses had before. He'd basically be thumbing his nose at them if he okayed the boat. Markham tipped his hand when he said he wished he had money left in the budget because the Eureka looked like something they *would have liked* to try."

Holland looked disgusted, "That's the same manure they've been throwing at us for the last eight years. There's never any money for Marine Corps needs."

"Well, we've got some naval personnel that went to bat for us. Goddard says to me, 'Mr. Higgins, could you build one like your drawing for $5200.00? I believe we have that much left in the budget that's not assigned.' He was nodding his head as he said it. I took it as a sign, which it was, and I said, 'I sure can.' You should have seen Markham's face. He turned so pale it looked like a vampire had been sucking on his neck. One of his staff remarked that $5,200 was one fifth of what they were spending for another design. That was good information for me, too. Ol' Markham didn't know what to say. He just sat there while his staff babbled on. I think he finally concluded he was stuck with approving it."

Smith visualized the drawings he'd seen earlier in the day. He asked, "Andrew, can you build one of those boats for that little amount of money? What I saw today looked like it would cost a lot more than $5,200."

"Hell, no! It will cost at least twice that to build. But the way I look at it, the money will be well spent. I know the Eureka is so much better than what they're considering, I'm sure to get a contract, eventually. If he offered to pay $1000, I'd still have agreed to it. I've invested too much time, effort and money over the past ten years, and, I know it's a sure thing. You never pass on a sure thing. I'll bet you I eventually build hundreds of these."

Their waiter arrived with the champagne, pouring each of them a full glass. Ada seemed so engrossed listening to the band she never turned to look at her drink. After asking Higgins if everything was satisfactory, the waiter wandered off leaving Smith and Higgins to return to their conversation.

Smith could see Higgins logic. "I'll take another look at those prints tomorrow. When do you think you'll have the prototype finished? I assume it will be the same as the drawings."

Andrew shook his head disgustedly. "No, it won't. Markham insisted that the boat be cut down to thirty feet, the engine be changed to one the Navy is currently using, and a lot of little things I'll call 'dirty drinking fountain gripes' rather than real changes. I asked why he wanted to cut the craft from thirty-eight to thirty feet, but I couldn't get a straight answer out of him. All he'd tell me was that thirty feet was a Navy requirement that couldn't be changed. The motor they want to put in is fine. It will necessitate a few engineering changes and will under-power the unit slightly, but it shouldn't impair the Eureka's performance."

"Damn it! We need those extra eight feet! What in hell are they thinking about?" Howlin' Mad's legendary anger made an instant appearance. "Let me write a let—"

"Don't you think it would be more prudent to let the first one be built the way the Navy has approved it, dear?" Ada interjected. She had been listening despite giving the appearance she was totally immersed in listening to the band. "After all, you've been pushing those people for the last five years and now you've got what you've wanted. It would seem that it might be better to ask for the changes after you try the first one."

Higgins laughed, "That's a good piece of advice for both of us. Holland, you have a very astute wife."

Ada smiled graciously. "Thank you, Mr. Higgins. And, oh yes, you were right about the band."

* * *

As the night came to a close, Ada and Holland drove back to their quarters. Ada broke the silence that had fallen over them since leaving Andrew Higgins at the hotel. "Andrew is quite an engaging fellow. He's fun to be around." Holland remained silent. Seemingly, he hadn't heard her. Ada looked at her husband, saw that he was deep in thought, but decided to interrupt anyway. "That tank is going to run over our rear end." She spoke loud enough to get his attention.

"What?" He was confused as he came back from the thought train on which he was traveling.

"You're not listening to me, Holland."

"I'm sorry. I was thinking about those Navy jackasses making changes to the Eureka before we even had a chance to test it. I'd like to—"

"Now, Holland, remember the advice General Russell gave you. And remember what you said Uncle John Milby used to tell you all the time about catching more flies with honey than vinegar. You got two things you've always wanted, an assignment that allows you to put into practice the visions you have for the Marines' tactics and now the go-ahead for developing and acquiring that landing craft you've told me you need desperately. You wouldn't want to endanger it by acting rashly."

"I need to remember that, dear. Sometimes I wish I had you in my pocket reminding me to keep control when I'm wrestling the Navy brass hats. Ada, there are a lot of good naval officers. Most, actually. There are just enough bureaucratic martinets in key positions to stifle the progress we want to make in the Corps. Hell, Ada, they do it to themselves. Naval aviation should be years ahead of where it is today. The old black shoe sailors won't give up the idea that battleships and surface actions are going to continue to determine who wins control of the sea. We should be building carriers twice as fast as other ships. And subs. Old ideas die hard."

"From what I heard the two of you talking about, it certainly seems that developing the Higgins boat will solve most of your landing craft problems."

"If Higgins' boat is successful, it will allow us to make great strides in amphibious warfare. Having a good piece of equipment like the Eureka allows us to get our men to shore quickly with a minimum of exposure to enemy fire," Holland hesitated and took a deep breath, "some of the time."

"What else do you need?"

"You heard us talking about the Christie tank?"

"Yes, but I didn't pay much attention."

"Well, a few years back the Navy tried to develop an amphibious tank. A man named Christie was the fellow who built the test units. The idea was to land these first to provide fire support for troops landing in boats. The realization that boats won't always be able to reach the shore means men will have to wade in through machine gun fire.

That's murderous. The tanks were to be used to suppress the enemy. Christie's tank had wheels and tracks like a bulldozer mounted on it. The tank floated and worked okay in smooth water, but it was a death trap in the surf. It would rollover or swamp. The Navy gave up on it. Vickers tried developing one, too. It was unsuccessful. That doesn't change the fact that the need is still there. There's going to be times when reefs, extremely shallow water, or places that are very heavily defended will create that need for a tank or something like it to keep our boys from being slaughtered. Even the Higgins boat won't solve that. We need something—that's armored, that we can mount machine guns and light cannons on—that can march across reefs and that can carry our guys up the beaches to cover. Unfortunately, I'm sure that the next place the Marines will fight is in the Pacific and these conditions will have to be faced repeatedly."

"Can Andrew add those things to his Eureka?"

"I talked to him about that. He says he can add armor and light weapons to his boats, but he doesn't see how he can modify it to be an amphibian."

"How are you going to solve that problem? It sounds like it may not be possible."

"Ada, I've told you the story of how John Milby came to live on our property when I was a boy. I spent more time with him growing up than I did with my school friends.

John was one of the closest friends I ever had. He taught me to hunt and fish, to ride horseback, and . . . more about human nature than I've learned from all the sources I've been exposed to in my life to date. John was a slave in his youth, he learned human relations to survive. When confronted with a difficult problem, his favorite saying was, 'You's cain't loads 'em wagons with da cotton, 'til you's pushes da first bale.' I have to push that bale."

Ada's tone was serious, "Diplomatically."

Holland grinned, "Diplomatically."

11

The Ugliest Side of War: The Rape of Nanking
1937, Nanking, China

The Mercedes drove down the rubble strewn streets, its diplomatic flags whipping in the wind. The cold air outside the car reduced, but did not eliminate, the smell of death. And, *death* filled the streets of Nanking. The swastikas on those flags were meant to insure the safety of the German embassy official that rode inside. Herr Manfred Von Dressell felt everything *but* safe. Events over the past several days were so dire he feared for his life and his wife's, who frightfully huddled inside the embassy.

This was his first excursion outside the German compound's protective walls since the Japanese had seized Nanking. He'd been told by Berlin to expect the Japanese to capture the city, China's capital, within weeks of the information being passed to him. The collapse of the Chinese army defending the city came sooner than he expected. While the Chinese troops fought hard, they had outmoded weapons, pitiful quantities of artillery, no air support, and lacked all supplies from food and ammunition to medical. In many cases, the Chinese were poorly trained and poorly led. They fought against some of the most dedicated, well trained and armed soldiers in the world in 1937. The result was inevitable.

Berlin swore to him that he and all embassy personnel would be perfectly safe. The Japanese had given assurances to the German government that his embassy would be given a wide berth. No bombs or artillery shells were supposed to land within 200 meters of the compound. His only responsibility was to be sure Fatherland's flag remained flying above the buildings. He kept his part of the agreement, the Japanese did not. Aircraft dropped bombs on the street in front of the embassy a scant thirty meters from the embassy's front door, shattering windows and dislodging books from shelves. Stray shells found their way into the grounds on three occasions, killing a maid and clerk on one of these instances. His wife remained petrified with fright for three days until the fighting past them.

Von Dressell had seen war before. He'd been in the lines at St. Lo and in the battle for the Ardennes during the Great War, or World War I as it was beginning to be known; he knew the staggering cost in lives and property a modern war demanded as its toll. Burning towns—refuges aimlessly searching for safe haven—widowed women crying—corpses torn to shreds, piled in heaps, decomposing—men screaming for help that wouldn't come—men like himself who were missing a hand, arm, leg, or suffering other disfigurements, men who would have to change their lives forever. Those were all memories he'd have just as soon forgotten, but as anyone who has been subjected to the horrors of battle, cannot.

But, he'd not seen war like the one broiling outside the auto he rode in. Von Dressell wondered if what he was witnessing could even be called war. It was massacre, slaughter and degradation being inflicted by one group of humans on another that was so vile it could not be believed. However, the reality of what he saw, heard and smelled were undeniable. Its shocking sights could not be fully described, but he knew he must try.

The Japanese had crushed Nanking's last defenses a few days before, capturing large numbers of Chinese troops. Resistance ended. Then, when the killing should have stopped, it began again, with a new viciousness and total disregard for human rights and dignity that he couldn't fully comprehend. The conquerors started satisfying their lust for blood and revenge by turning their rage on the hapless prisoners of war. Large numbers of POWs required too many Japanese troops to control them. Food and medicine were in short supply. It was easier to kill, than to care for, the captured men.

The first reports filtering into the haven the cloistered embassy provided were shocking. These stories were rumors of mass shootings of Chinese troops held in prisoner compounds. Trucks with canvas sides, backs, and tops had

Nambu machine guns set up in the rear manned by crews ready to shoot. These vehicles would back up to enclosures housing POWs. When the trucks were in position, the back and sides were lifted, then the gunners sprayed the helpless prisoners with withering machine gun fire. They continued to shoot until there was no movement.

Once the decision to eradicate the prisoners was sanctioned, all sense of humanity seemed to flee from large segments of the Japanese soldiers and officers. Using the Japanese value system of the time, the ultimate disgrace for a soldier was for him to surrender. He became a non-entity. The conquering troops used this ruler to measure those taken prisoner. Their lives were valueless and the Japanese treated them as such. Von Dressell had heard of two Jap officers who staged a contest to see which could behead the most prisoners with his sword in one minute. The winner was reported to have slain 102. Manfred dismissed the report as a myth until photographs of the barbaric event found their way to his desk. One picture showed the winning officer standing behind a long line of heads, his bloody sword held menacingly outward over the gruesome trophies. One foot rested on a severed head, the officer smiled proudly. The prisoners became targets for bayonet practice; they were gutted and hung from trees upside-down, buried alive, beaten to death, burned to death, pulled apart by vehicles moving in opposite directions and other cruel methods of murder.

The Japanese troops' focus enlarged to include the civilian population. Pillaging, raping, and burning quickly lost interest for the unrestrained soldiers. Killing civilians started slowly for a day or two, then grew into complete, unrestrained butchery. Men, women and children were selected at random, killed and mutilated, creating scenes beyond belief. Women became the focus of the soldiers, rape being so common few escaped it. Many were raped so many times they lost count. Some were held as prisoners so they could be raped and assaulted at the pleasure of their tormentors. When the Japs finished with their victims, the women were killed or tortured, maimed and further defiled. The lucky ones received a simple bullet to the brain.

The Mercedes wove around abandoned materials left by fleeing refugees as they realized any impediment to their immediate effort to evade the marauding troops might well mean death or worse. The car passed burning buildings that mixed acrid smells of wood smoke with the sickly sweet stench of human decay. The car swerved to avoid a dead boy of six lying face up in a pool of blood that had come from a wound in his chest. Von Drussell's eyes went from one terrifying sight to another. Two women's bodies lay on the side of the street, evidently shot while running for safety. In the next block, an old man, probably the butcher shop's proprietor, hung from the store's sign, a meat hook driven into his neck and tied to the rope suspending him. A bayoneted young girl lay on the street's edge, naked from the waist down, her unseeing eyes staring at the car. Another block produced another ghastly vision. Two bodies so hacked apart it was impossible to even tell their gender, lay decomposing on the curb. The German closed his eyes, he'd seen enough.

Von Dressell spoke to his driver. "Hans, get back to the compound as quickly as possible. I've decided to cancel my visit to the Swiss. I'll send my message by courier if the phones aren't working. This is too much to bear."

"Gladly, Herr Von Dressell!" The relieved driver made two quick right turns onto a street paralleling the one that had the horrible sights adorning it, and traveled back to the embassy and its relative safety. After traveling two blocks without passing a disgusting corpse, Manfred sighed; hopefully he would be spared any more such sights. He shook his head. If what he was seeing and had heard was indicative of Japanese moral values and culture, how could the Fuhrer consider an alliance with such people? Certainly the Fatherland's great leader didn't know of his proposed allies' barbarity. No civilized human being could condone these acts. Von Dressell's four year stay in China had fostered a fondness for the Chinese. He resolved to gather as much evidence of the atrocities occurring in Nanking that he could and present them to the Foreign Service when he returned to Germany in a few weeks. He was being recalled because of some mysterious problem in his wife's family. Manfred couldn't imagine why. Herr and Frau Goldman were the most retiring, non-controversial people he knew. The Goldmans had friends in the German government that they were confident would protect them from complications due to their Jewish heritage, which they had abandoned years before.

"Look," Hans said. "I've heard they're doing that, but it's the first time I actually saw it."

"What, Hans?"

"Look up the street, on the left." Hans pointed at something on the roadside a block ahead.

"I don't see what you're looking at"

"The women tied over the crate." Hans pointed again. "See her now?"

Von Dressell concentrated on the area his driver motioned toward. He finally saw what Hans was talking about. A woman was bent over a large wooden box at the waist. She was completely naked. As the car approached, Manfred saw that her legs were spread wide apart and tied to the crate's bottom. Her stomach and chest were flat on the top of the box; her arms were stretched downward and tied to the crate's bottom. Her body formed a "U" with her buttocks prominently exposed. "My God! Hans are they doing to that woman what I think they are?"

"If you think rape, yes." Hans glanced over his shoulder. "The troops call them women of convenience. One of our *Wehrmacht* guards speaks Japanese fluently. He told me he spoke to one of their officers. Supposedly, these women are being punished and made an example because they have committed some act against the troops. If any soldier passes, he is encouraged to rape her."

"What happens to them? The women?" Von Dressel was incredulous.

Hans kept his eyes on the road, but took one index finger and passed it across his throat in a slitting motion. The car had reached the woman. Von Dressell could see wounds on her back, blood was caked on her back, rear, and legs, and he heard her cry out as they passed. He yelled, "Stop the car!"

Manfred had the door open before the vehicle halted completely. He searched his pants and coat for the pocket knife he normally carried as he rushed over to the victim. The knife wasn't to be found. The woman was crying and talking incoherently. He said in Mandarin, "I will help you." He knelt down to untie the rope holding her hands to the box. As he fumbled with the knots with his only hand, Hans screamed, "Herr Von Dressell, soldiers!" He heard them yelling as he straightened up. Two infantrymen had emerged from a building and were racing at him with fixed bayonets. He folded his arms and tried to stare them down.

They didn't even slow down until a strong voice barked a command from behind the two privates. The two men froze, but kept their Ansaki rifles pointed at Von Dressell.

A small man wearing an Imperial Army officer's cap walked up from behind the privates. He carefully examined the car, taking note of the flags, then turned his attention to Von Dressell. Other soldiers exited from buildings lining the streets and moved toward the car until one curt word from the officer halted them abruptly. The major stopped when he was two paces from Manfred. He said something in Japanese Von Dressell didn't understand.

Von Dressell spoke in German, "I don't speak Japanese."

"Nine sprechenze Duetsch," the officer answered. He raised his eyebrows and said, "You speak Engrish."

"A little," Von Dressell replied.

They stood silently, looking at each other with harsh eyes, each trying to decide what to do next. Finally, the major said, "Not good for you here. You go 'way."

"I cannot. That woman is being mistreated. I intend to free her." Von Dressell pointed at the woman.

"You go 'way," the officer repeated, but with a sterner tone.

"I'm going to free her." Von Dressell raised his voice to match the major's forcefulness.

"No. Woman not respect Japan sordier. Spit on sordier.

Say bad thing 'bout Japan and Japan sordier. In East, no roose face is important." The major was trying to remain cool.

As Manfred bent over to untie the woman he said, "I'm freeing this woman. She's not an animal."

The major yelled a command and troops immediately surrounded the Mercedes. The two privates lunged forward and held their bayonets inches from Von Dressell's face. The officer spoke very calmly, "You go now."

"As soon as I let her——" As Manfred started to kneel, one of the privates held his bayonet to Von Dressell's throat, pressing right to the point of penetration.

"You touch woman, you die!" There was no indecision in the major's voice.

"My driver will report what happens here. You'll be court-martialed." Von Dressell hoped his bluff would work.

The major raised his head back slightly and squinted his eyes. "Driver die, too. Bad Chinee kirr both yous. Our sordier witness." He leaned forward onto his toes. "You go NOW!"

"Please, Herr Von Dressell!" Hans pleaded from the car.

Manfred hesitated. The officer would do as he threatened. His and Han's deaths would be wasted in a futile attempt to free the victim and would do nothing to help the woman. He straightened up and looked into the major's eyes. There was no pity, compassion, fear or indecisiveness there. Von Dressell would do what he could. "I'm a member of the German government. I request you release this woman and take care of her."

"I see frag," the officer pointed to the car. "I take care of woman. You go NOW!"

Von Dressell walked back to the car. As he opened the rear car door, the major said something in Japanese and the troops hooted. Manfred said, "Hans, let's get back to the embassy quickly."

As they drove away, the woman screamed. Von Dressell did not look back. He asked Hans, "You know some Japanese, what did the officer say as I got back in the car?"

"See men, all whites are inferior cowards before Japanese strength."

Von Dressell's humiliation was complete. He thought, *I'll be happy to be back in Germany in a few weeks where there isn't this barbarity.*

12

Cocktails and Coincidence – Christmas 1937, San Diego, California

"Merry Christmas, General," Rear Admiral Edward C. Kalbfus greeted his Marine colleague with a big smile as he entered the room. The two men exchanged cordial, casual salutes.

Major General Louis M. Little returned the smile and said, "Thank you and a Merry Christmas to you, Eddie. And, I'll even add a Happy New Year to that."

"I'll call your Happy New Year, Louis. Let's wander over to the bar and drink to that." The poker playing men laughed and headed for the mahogany. After receiving their drinks from a stolid bar-tender, the two officers scanned the room until they found an unoccupied corner housing a comfortable looking sofa with a convenient coffee table placed in front of it. After sitting down, Rear Admiral Kalbfus raised his glass and said, "To the Navy and the Corps."

"To the Navy and the Corps," General Little agreed.

The two men took a sip of their cocktails. Kalbfus said, "It doesn't seem like Christmas in Dago, does it. The temperature is seventy-one out there. We'd be a lot more comfortable in dungarees and undershirts than these." He stuck a thumb into his dress uniform shirt-front and pulled out. "I guess it beats being in Pearl or Cavite for the holidays. At least there are decorations in the department stores and Christmas songs on the radio. You ever hear *Jingle Bells* played on a Hawaiian steel guitar and sung by Polynesian girls in grass skirts? It loses the spirit of the season."

They both laughed. "To the Navy and the Corps," General Little repeated and each took another drink.

Kalbfus said, "I hope both the Navy and the Corps have that Happy New Year we just wished for each other."

"I think we will, Eddie." The General was puzzled.

"I hope you're right, Louis. I'm just not too sure we won't be in a war by the end of this year." The Admiral took another sip of his drink. He gently shook the glass back and forth, clinking the ice cubes inside. "The way things are going in Europe and in China—well, it looks pretty dim. I heard Nanking fell on the 13th. When the Japanese finish that campaign, they'll control almost all of China's industrialized area and 70% of the best agricultural lands. I can't help but wonder where they'll go next. I'm guessing Indo-China."

"You see any of the intelligence reports on the Nanking thing?"

"No, not the actual reports, but I heard it was bad."

Little shook his head, "Bad doesn't come close. It was

horrible butchery. The Japanese committed atrocities that were so wide spread the report I saw said that half the Imperial Army should be prosecuted. What they did to the civilians . . . ," he shook his head again, "they're heartless bastards. I feel sorry for those folks in Indo-China if they're next. Think the French would go to war with Japan over that?"

"I don't know. With Hitler rattling his saber right next door, that's a hell of a long way from Europe to fight a war." Kalbfus hesitated, then added, "Think we might get the call to help?"

"I heard the State Department and Cordell Hull are doing their best to keep the Japs out of there. They're threatening them with sanctions." The General set his glass on the table. "I know our planning people are taking another look at the Orange Plan and updating it. Whether we'd do it to defend the French . . . I don't think so, but you don't know." He looked at the Admiral and said deliberately, "You know, Eddie, as much as any of us don't want a war, we're paid to fight them."

"That's our job. But, the way things look in the world today . . . ." Kalbfus shook his head. "We might end up fighting a two front war. Hitler keeps pushing for expansion. Mussolini keeps beating his gums, though from what I've read, he's still fighting in Ethiopia. Hitler's thumbed his nose at most of the military restrictions in the Versailles treaty. The French are beefing up the Maginot Line. Hitler keeps demanding the Sudetenland be ceded back to Germany. It could blow up."

"I don't think we have to worry about the Krauts for another year or two." Little leaned forward. "First, the French didn't do a thing when Hitler reoccupied the Rhineland last year. If they wouldn't stop Hitler then, I guarantee they won't do anything to save the Sudetenland for the Czechoslovakians. The French won't go it alone. Second, the new British Prime Minister, Neville Chamberlain, doesn't want any part of a war. From what I've heard about him, he'd give his wife to Hitler as a whore to stay out of another war with Germany. Besides, the British are more scared of the Soviets than they are the Nazi's. The British would like to see those two fight it out amongst each other." Little picked up his glass and took a drink. He frowned, "As long as the same fellow's tending bar, we won't have to worry about getting drunk." Louis put his glass down. "If we go to war this year, I'm betting it's with Japan."

"You're not concerned about the Anti-Commintern Pact Berlin and Tokyo signed last month?" the Admiral asked. "It looks to me as if that agreement is designed to give the Japanese a free hand in the Pacific."

"Yes it does, but it's pointed at the Soviets. Hitler wants the threat of Japan beating up on the Russians rear and dividing the Soviet forces if he gets into a war in Europe. It doesn't mean Hitler is going to declare war on us if the Japs do it first. He might, however, if we declare war on Japan first. It depends on how strong Hitler thinks he is. I don't think he's willing to take on Britain, France, the Soviets and the U.S. right now. The trouble with all these alliances, pacts and sanctions are that they eventually force somebody's hand. It's like the Abyssinian crises. Italy was in the process of forming an alliance with France and Britain until Anthony Eden threatened Mussolini with oil sanctions. Now the bastard's lining up with Hitler." Little reflected for a few seconds. "I guess Hitler *might* declare war on us because of the Pact. But, I still think if war comes this year, my money's on the Japanese—with Hitler sitting it out. As long as the Russians are a threat, he's very vulnerable. The Soviets have the world's largest Army by far, as well as the largest Air Force. Hitler doesn't do anything that works to his disadvantage."

"Louis, I sure hope you're wrong about the possibility of war with the Japanese this coming year. We aren't ready. Period. I think we're strong enough to meet their fleet. The only category of ships we wouldn't have superiority in is carriers and naval air power hasn't proven itself yet." Admiral Kalbfus shook his head. "The problem is distance. The war is likely to take place in French Indochina, Malaysia and the Dutch East Indies. The supply line to our bases in the Philippines is very vulnerable. We'll need bases all across the central Pacific. The Japs have all those islands now. That means *your boys* have to make a lot of landings on fortified islands to take them away." Kalbfus snapped his fingers. "That reminds me, Louis, have you seen the October 4th issue of Life Magazine?"

"No. I don't believe I have."

Kalbfus stood up. "Lou, will you excuse me for a few seconds? I think I saw a copy of that issue by the entrance where we came in. There's something in it you should see."

"Go right ahead." General Little stood and said, "While you're magazine hunting, I'll head back to the bar and get us both a refill."

When General Little returned, Ed Kalbfus was waiting, a smile on his face that would make a Cheshire Cat envious. He held the issue of Life he wanted. The magazine was folded to the article he wanted Little to see. "I've been involved in some of the Fleet Landing Exercises and I know that you Marines aren't satisfied with the boats you're using. The Colonel who is in charge of Planning and Training in Washington is always pushing for an improved landing craft. What's his name, I forget? Screaming Mad?"

"It's Holland M. Smith. But, most people call him Howlin' Mad Smith. He's a very good man, but he can be a pain in the ass."

"When I saw this, I thought of you fellows and one of

Howlin' Mad's letters I read. Anyway, take a look at it." Admiral Kalbfus handed the folded Life Magazine to General Little.

Little read the title aloud, "Roebling's Alligator for Florida Hurricane Rescues." When his eyes focused on the pictures, his jaw clamped shut, his face flushed and he eased down onto the sofa. The pictures featured a large vehicle that looked like a military tank with the turret removed, the inside gutted and then converted to open hauling space. A trapezoid was formed by the treads and their suspension system. One picture showed the vehicle filled with men as it made its way across a bay. Another showcased the amphibian's ability to crash through obstacles as it drove through a mangrove forest.

The caption under this photo read, "The Alligator is virtually unstoppable, grinding whole trees and shrubs to matchwood." Superlative language in the article praised the seaworthiness of the amphibian, its ease of operation and maneuverability, rugged construction and exceptional durability. Specifications for the unit were also very impressive. Weight – 8,700 pounds. Capacity – 40 men. Land Speed – 18 mph. Water Speed – 8.6 mph. All metal construction. General Little looked up at Ed Kalbfus and said, "Impressive, very impressive. I hope these people don't mind me stealing their magazine." Little extended his hand to his friend, the Admiral. "Thanks, Ed. This is very exciting. I'm going to do a little checking and send this on to Commandant Holcomb. This may be the answer we've been looking for."

13

Unveiling a Masterpiece – Don Roebling
1938, Don Roebling
Clearwater Bay, Florida

"I didn't think it got cold down here." Major John Kaluf hunched his shoulders as a cold breeze blew against his neck. The bright Florida sun beat down on the wind chilled aluminum interior of the amphibious tractor that housed Kaluf, Donald Roebling, Warren Cottrell, and Kaluf's aide, Corporal Jensen. All four huddled behind the raised silhouette of the driver's cab to reduce the penetrating cold.

"Oh, it gets cold down here sometimes." Donald Roebling wet his finger and held it up in the wind. "It's coming out of the Northwest. Good, that should give us higher waves over on the beach for the demonstration." Roebling's voice had an excitement in it that couldn't be masked. Ten weeks before, Donald had been hard at work trying to convince the State of Florida and the Red Cross of the viability of purchasing and using his Alligator as a primary rescue vehicle for hurricane relief. Then, during the first week of February, a lightning bolt descended. Not from the sky—from Washington, D.C. It came in the form

of a request from the US Marine Corps for information regarding his amphibious vehicle. Roebling was shocked,
flattered and deliriously happy. He mounted a Herculean
effort, answering all the questions posed in the Marine in-
quiry, volunteering additional information he felt would be
helpful. He designed, wrote and had printed a color bro-
chure, volunteered his vehicle for inspection/test operation,
and had everything in the hands of the officer making the
request in five days. The Marines were impressed by Roebling's presentation.

Meeting Don Roebling for the first time had created
some apprehension for Kaluf. The inventor's pride, effu-
sive personality, and the claims Roebling made before
they'd even viewed the unit concerned the Marine officer.
A quick walk around the vehicle and discussions with the
technicians, Cottrell, Be Bolt and Williams, dispelled that.
The ruggedly built vehicle was twenty-one feet long and
nine feet wide, looked like it could carry the twenty soldiers and their equipment Roebling claimed it could, and
reminded him of the light tanks already used by the Corps.

Major Kaluf was even more impressed with the Alligator after his first day of inspection. Roaring into the water
through tangles of grass and other vegetation, and quickly
stabilizing in Panther Marsh's waters had left a great first
impression. Alternately running through deep mud and
swimming around the swamp, going to any area the major

wished, combined with the vehicles ability to transverse obstacles like small logs with no hiccups, excited him. Told to stand on a platform in the cargo area of the vehicle, Kaluf swallowed hard when one of the techs opened a valve allowing water to pour into the craft. He was equally flabbergasted to see the Alligator maintain its buoyancy as it pumped out water faster than it entered. It was as maneuverable and reached the speeds Roebling claimed it would. Having a piece of equipment do precisely as advertised was, indeed, rare.

"Take her out, Warren." Roebling practically bubbled as he spoke with a dramatic flair. He knew the previous day's tests in Panther Marsh had fascinated the Marine officer. He knew what he'd planned for the second demonstration was spectacular.

The engine roared and Cottrell shifted the unit into gear, its specially designed tracks clawing at the sand as it drove the fifty yards from its parking place to Clearwater Bay. The Alligator entered the water at its full speed of 18 mph, sending showers of spray into the air from the gently deepening, shallow water.

Kaluf smiled, "Fantastic, Roebling, fantastic." The Major was a good judge of human character and was aware of Roebling's pride in his invention and the potential benefit of stroking it. "I can visualize the Alligator landing on beaches and crossing rivers, packed with our men, saving countless lives."

"John—Major do you mind if I call you John?" Don
asked.

"Hell no, I'd prefer it."

"Good! John, you haven't seen anything yet. No sir, not
anything." Roebling tapped Cottrell on the shoulder and
said, "Warren, take the Alligator over to the place we discussed."

Cottrell corrected the craft's direction sixty degrees and
pointed the bow toward a mangrove covered shoreline and
directly into the whitecaps formed by the twenty knot wind.
The Alligator dropped deeper into the water until the cleats
on the treads no longer contacted the bottom, effectively
converting the tractor to a boat. It glided to its water speed
of 8.5 mph. Churning out the back were two wakes created
by the cupped devices mounted to every track tread. These
"paddles" tossed water a foot-and-a-half into the air behind
the Alligator.

"We're floating now?" Kaluf asked.

"Yes, we're buoyant. Yes, we're afloat." Roebling's
tendency was to repeat himself when he was excited. A
wave crashed into the bow sending spray over the front and
dampening the vessel's occupants. "Don't worry about the
spray. We can make the shield higher. It could be increased
by a foot or more. And, as you know, the Alligator has
pumps built in."

"The spray isn't a factor at all," Kaluf said, while making a mental note that increasing the shield height slightly, with the proper material, would provide additional protection for the troops inside. "How deep is this bay?"

"Right here we're in about eight feet. These bays aren't very deep; the most we'll have under us is around fourteen or so." Roebling pointed across the bay. "There's a place over on that shore we can cross and go out into the Gulf. With this wind, we should have four foot of surf. We'll take the Alligator any place you want to take her, John."

Cottrell winced. He hoped his boss's mouth didn't create problems for them. Every machine has its limits and Warren was aware of the Alligator's.

The tractor cruised across the bay negotiating the heavy chop with ease. As they plowed through the waves, Kaluf removed a small notebook from his pocket and scribbled a few notes. Roebling watched him intensely.

"You said the top speed in water is 8 plus mph?" Kaluf asked.

"Yes, that's correct. That's correct." Don tried to change the subject, being concerned that the speed might not be great enough. "See that area over there?" Roebling wiggled his arm at another portion of the bay. "That's very good trout and redfish water. Come down again and we'll see you get into the fish." Roebling looked like a young child offering his best toy to a prospective friend as an enticement.

Kaluf grinned and said, "Okay."

Roebling looked at the mangroves that formed a seemingly impenetrable wall on the shore, now a couple hundred
yards away. He said, "John, behind the trees on that shore
there are more small bays and creeks. Point to a spot. Point
to a spot."

"Okay." Kaluf extended his arm and index finger at a
spot thirty degrees to the right of the Alligator's current
course.

"Warren," Roebling said. Cottrell glanced at Kaluf, adjusted some levers and the craft smoothly shifted its heading to the place Kaluf indicated. "*Now,* you'll see what the
Alligator can do," Don added.

The Alligator's treads touched the bottom when the
craft was thirty yards from the bank. Warren reduced the
speed to half its capability as the amphibian gradually rose
from the water. Kaluf gasped and braced himself as the
tractor plowed on toward the scraggly mangroves now only
a few yards away. The treads ground into the spreading
stilts of the trees root system while the vehicle's front
swept the foliage, limbs and trunks aside and under the
tractor. Kaluf's and his corporal's eyes widened with aston-
ishment as the Alligator tore a path through the thick brush
and trees. After clearing a "road" for 25 yards, the tractor
emerged from the mangroves and splashed into the shallow

water of a small bay, leaving crushed and fractured wood less than two feet high behind.

Jensen whistled and said, "Wow!"

Kaluf added, "Absolutely incredible!"

Warren Cottrell sighed with relief.

* * *

"Would you like some more wine?" John Roebling asked John Kaluf. The Roeblings, Don and his father John, Major Kaluf and Corporal Jensen sat around a table at one of the finest restaurants on the West Coast of Florida. A waiter stood in readiness to serve the table's occupants' slightest whim. He did so happily—he was experienced in serving the Roeblings *and* knew their generosity in such circumstances. The remainders of perfectly prepared steaks dotted the four men's plates who were celebrating four successful days of tests and inspection of the Alligator.

"No, thank you, Mr. Roebling. I've had all I can eat or drink. I'm stuffed. That was the best meal I've had in ages." Kaluf eased away from the table. Everyone had finished eating with the exception of Don Roebling, who was in the act of eating chocolate pie—a whole one.

"Are you sure? Are you sure?" Roebling asked.

"No. If I ate another bite, I wouldn't be able to leave the table."

"I hope you feel your trip was worth your effort," Don said, fishing for one more repeat of the praise already heaped on his invention.

"Your unit met or far exceeded our expectations. We'd need some minor changes to your design to test it for combat, things like a place to mount a machine gun, maybe add some armor, but you've designed a truly exceptional and revolutionary vehicle."

"Thank you, again. Thank you."

Kaluf said, "No, I want to thank you both for your cooperation and hospitality during our visit here. Particularly for repeating the outstanding demonstrations you did the previous days so we could film the Alligator's operation. I'm sure that the effort will pay off for you in the future."

Roebling abruptly dropped his fork on his plate, making a clinking sound. "Major Kaluf, I can assure you that our primary interest in developing the Alligator is to help save lives, not to sell it for profit. If the Alligator would help the Marines land safely and reduce the number of our men killed, we would consider that highest payment. Right, father?"

"Absolutely, Don."

Kaluf looked at the father and son incredulously. It was hard to believe that these men were driven by service to country more strongly than to service of self. However, based on his last four days in Clearwater, it was difficult to dispute the two men's statements and intentions. They had even offered to make the modifications to the tractor to make it more battle worthy *at no charge*. They had been ready to allow the Marines to test the unit; Kaluf had to explain he'd have to gain approval *and* dissuade them from voluntarily shipping the Alligator and an accompanying technician to a Marine base, at the Roeblings' expense. After a few added seconds of contemplation, the Major spoke in carefully measured words, "I can only say to both of you that your efforts here may do just that. My report will recommend we support a trial of the Alligator. You can be assured it will be recommended in the highest possible manner. Your invention is one of the most remarkable I've seen and I believe it will do more to save Marine lives than any piece of equipment ever developed." Kaluf was pleased with the expressions on both Roeblings' faces. There was fierce pride and unmasked pleasure taken from his remarks.

"Gentlemen, we must toast the Major's words." John Roebling motioned to the waiter and said, "Andrew, please bring us a bottle of your best champagne." Emotion vibrated in his voice.

Kaluf saw tears on Don Roebling's cheek as Don added, "Yes, we need a toast." The major thought, *I believe these men may be sincere!*

Don broke the spell when he called after the waiter, "Andrew, would you bring another one of these pies for me. Thanks."

14

Dress Rehearsal for Death and a Possible Savior
1938, Holland Smith
Island of Culebra, the Caribbean

Motor launches churned away for the white sands. The boats were the latest menagerie of craft provided by the Bureau of Ships to solve the Marine Corps requirements for equipment suitable to assault a fortified beach. A small Navy cutter lay anchored three miles off the beach and would act as the line of departure marker, that invisible boundary between reason and civility and the Marines entrance into barbarous hell. The craft simultaneously changed course to one paralleling Culebra's coast line. They assembled at a point seaward of the cutter and divided into two equal groups, each group forming a circle. The boats maintained even distances between them. All boats followed the craft's stern in front of its bow, like a pack of wolves with each individual chasing the tail of the animal ahead.

"They aren't lined up correctly, Colonel. The rear group is twenty degrees off of the approach line." A major in the officer group observing and monitoring the practice looked at Smith. "Want me to signal them to make the correction?"

Colonel Holland Smith sighed deeply. They hadn't even started for the beach and there was already a disruption in the plan and time table. The imaginary naval bombardment's timing relative to the crafts approach to the shore was critical. Any deviation would have deadly consequences for the Marines attacking the beach. "No. They'll have to make the adjustment as they form the two waves."

The boats rode their invisible merry-go-round waiting for a signal. It came when two red flares burned in the sky simultaneous with a series of flags raised on the cutter's mast and two blasts of an air horn that came from the same ship's bridge. Immediately, the lead ship in each formation broke the circle and formed a line parallel with the line of departure. The first line of landing craft all turned at the same time. When all eight craft were in line, gunwale to gunwale, they headed for the shore. The line behind tried to execute the same maneuver and catch up with the lag in spacing at the same time. Smith shook his head.

Both lines of boats rushed for the shore. As the first group passed the cutter, the ship's crew responded by launching a single green flare, changing the flags on the mast, and sending a long blast from the air horn racing over the waters. When the second group passed the departure line the cutter repeated its signaling procedure. "How much of a delay?" Smith asked.

"About 116 seconds, sir. And they still aren't lined up completely right," the major answered.

Smith snorted and wrote several notes on a pad.

Ahead of the troops loomed the tropical island, four feet of surf crashing on its shores. Palm trees and the lush green hills behind the beaches were a vacationer's holiday vision. The 200 plus Marines packed into the boats carrying them to the sand weren't training for a pleasant dream. Their endeavor was preparation for a nightmare. The company sized force was a test for full scale practice landings that would follow. As the first wave closed on the shore, it was clear there would be problems. The line broke when some craft had to change course to avoid rocks and the reef. Instead of one solid line of boats unloading their troops at the same time, they approached in an uneven gaggle allowing an enemy to concentrate on one unloading boat at a time. The boats wallowed in the surf as the men struggled over the sides and raced up the beach. After the boats unloaded, they tried to break away from the sand. Only two were able to depart. The rest cluttered the landing area, barring the second wave from reaching their proper spots. Those boats milled about looking for the opportunity to land at or close to their assigned position. Any hope of a smooth operation was dead. Holland muttered, "Damned boats. The Bureau idiots are . . . ." He wrote a paragraph on his pad.

The Marines milled around on the beach, trying to execute the plan as devised. The chaos at the surf's edge made a shambles of orders. The men struggled to get the beached landing craft off the sand so other craft could land. Officers raced around trying to salvage the rehearsal. "H plus twenty minutes," the major on his staff informed.

"Get the men off the damned beach!" Smith roared. He watched disgustedly as the circus continued. After several more infuriating moments, Howlin' Mad roared. "This is shit! Against any reasonably deployed and trained troops we'd have a seventy percent casualty rate. Maybe a hundred. We can't live with those damned boats!"

* * *

"How would you rate your performance?" Holland Smith had a scowl on his face. He wasn't happy with the test of Marine battle tactics he'd just witnessed. Certainly the landing craft had started the plan on a ruinous path, but the lack of what he saw as effort and leadership after hitting the beach further incurred his wrath. That company sized exercise was pre-planning for Fleet Exercise 4 or, as the Navy shortened to an acronym, FLEX (#4). A sweating group of Marine officers stood in a circle around the colonel. Everyone remained silent. This further enraged Howlin' Mad. "Damn it, gentlemen, when I ask a question I expect an answer."

The captain in command of the company looked at Smith and shook his head, "I'll answer it the best I can, Colonel. What we accomplished stunk. The effort we expended was excellent."

"Captain, I want you to remember that when you're writing letters to parents and wives of young men *you* helped kill on the beach because you weren't able to get those boys off of it quickly enough to prevent a slaughter." Smith's face showed his displeasure.

"Sir, I followed the operational plans *exactly*. I was acutely aware that the time table we were supposed to be keeping was destroyed." The captain made a concerted effort to maintain his composure. "When the boats straggled to the beach, we didn't have a chance of executing our orders. The amount of time it took to get out of the boats is far greater than was planned. Our ammunition and supplies took forever to get to the beach, unloaded and delivered to us. From that point on, things compounded."

"Shit, Captain, I've got eyes. I'm not upset with the way that portion of the exercise occurred. I know that we're operating under a large handicap. The boats are crap. That doesn't change things. The objective is to get the men off that beach as quickly as possible."

The Captain looked exasperated. "Colonel Smith, we tried to move as fast as we could and stay within our orders. Everybody on the…"

"Damn it, Captain, that's what I'm most upset with. If your orders told you to put your mouth on the muzzle of a Browning 50 caliber and have one of your men thumb the triggers, would you? Show initiative. You know what the objective is, go after it!" Howlin' Mad's eyes flashed and his voice quavered.

"If you want us to act on our own initiative, why do we have such detailed orders? Most of us would have gotten the men we commanded off the beach, sir, like we've been trained. I know I would have. But, the orders we got were very specific. Get a minimum amount of munitions to the staging points before we allow others to safe-guard it. Get platoons organized or reorganized to minimum strength before the move in. If we don't follow them, aren't we in jeopardy of endangering the troops that aren't in our command. Or . . . ," the lieutenant hesitated.

Smith looked surprised, as though some monumental truth had been unveiled to him. After a few seconds of silence, he said calmly, "Go ahead, lieutenant."

"Well, sir, if we knowingly disobey orders, aren't we also in danger of reprimand or court martial?"

"I can tell you what you should do. I can't tell you that it will always be what your orders require." Holland Smith wasn't Howlin' Mad any more. "Your first responsibility is to take the objective you've been assigned. Your second responsibility is to your men. Your third responsibility is to your formal orders. Sometimes that means you have to rely on your leadership ability and training to make the right decision. In battle, the right answer isn't always in your orders or the safe one." Smith looked at the man patiently and asked, "What's your name?"

"Lieutenant Dave Shoup, sir."

Holland looked at the man, nodded, and said softly, "You've given me something to ponder." Smith turned back to the captain. "My point, Captain, is that the objective of getting the men off the beach is the most important. You can't carry out orders with dead men."

"Colonel, I'll remember that and act accordingly." The captain shook his head. "Sir, is there any hope of getting decent landing craft for us?"

Smith took a deep breath. "I'd like to tell you we have the problem solved. I can't. However, there is hope. We'll have a new style boat to test in the next few months. It's built by a manufacturer in New Orleans. It looks very good."

"Will it clear reefs like the one some of our boats had to maneuver around? That killed the timing of the landing waves."

Holland hesitated a few seconds, "No, Captain, not in every instance. When the Higgins boat is fully loaded, it draws nearly four feet at the stern. Higgins says it can get its bow right onto the beach, then retract from it. That's a great improvement. But, it won't solve every problem."

* * *

Weeks later in Smith's office, Washington DC

"I read your notes on the rehearsal for FLEX #4, Holland." Major General Thomas Holcomb smiled at Smith in a way Holland had never seen before. "You gave the company participating in the exercise a decent review. I agree with your comment on officer initiative and on the restructuring of plans to make them more flexible to meet the actual conditions faced on the beach. Most of the lack of effectiveness started right after leaving the departure line. You've concluded is due to the lack of proper landing craft to allow us to land an effective force as we must to keep losses to a minimum. I agree, particularly after looking at the films. You've asked where the Higgins' boat stands. Well, I got some good news. The funds passed the Navy Budget Officer's review. Higgins has the PO for the prototype."

"That is great news." Smith returned Holcomb's smile. "When do we get the boat to test?"

"Higgins is just getting approval to go ahead. I'm sure he'll give us a date as soon as he can. I'd guess late this fall." Holcomb stood by Smith's desk as though courting a conversation, unusual behavior for him.

"Good. I just hope we can get the Eureka operable and get enough action-ready before the Pacific boils over. Maybe we can expedite that late fall date some."

"Maybe. Holland, have you read the latest intelligence on the Nanking incident?"

"Yes, sir. That's a human travesty. The reports I've read claim the Japanese have killed up to 300,000 Chinese there. Two-thirds of them were civilians. I can't believe the way they brutalize women and children. The behavior of the average Imperial Japanese soldier and their officers is despicable if only ten percent of what I've read is true."

Holcomb folded his arms. "We're going to be fighting those people, and soon. Despite the politicians that want to be ostriches and bury their heads in the sand, war with Japan isn't avoidable, as I see it. You heard about Joe Taussig?"

"Yes, sir. That congressional committee sure didn't respect his Rear Admiral's stars. They couldn't stand to hear the truth. Taussig told them how it is. He predicted a war with Japan and that we need to fortify our Pacific bases to prevent the Japs from over-running them. Manila, Guam, Wake, Midway—they're all vulnerable. With the exception of the Philippines, a couple regiments of Japs could take Wake, Guam, or Midway. Hell, Saipan is a major base for them. Guam's within range of their land-based aircraft and we couldn't do a thing to help the small garrisons there. They didn't want to hear that. They didn't even want to believe that the Japanese are preparing for war with us despite all the evidence he offered. Now he's got half those congressmen, a bunch of half-assed newspapers and every pacifist screwball in the country screaming for his court-martial."

"Those people believe Chamberlain has the right idea. He keeps giving in to Hitler. Appeasement is what the papers are calling it." Holcomb sighed, "Sooner or later the British and French will run out of things they say he can take. When you're dealing with someone like Hitler or Tojo, they keep pushing until they force you into a war or you give them everything, including your soul."

Smith folded his hands and rested them on his desk. "Sir, Americans have a problem believing that other cultures have different definitions for what's fair, or humane, or ethical, or what a human life is worth. I could go on. We can't believe it when the Asians slaughter each other in merciless fashion. But I've been in the Orient enough to know the way we value one life is much different than the way Japanese or Chinese do. I guess every culture makes that mistake—believing the people they're confronting share the same values." He balled up his fists and tapped them lightly on his desk top. "We're looking at a brutal, no quarter war. If we're forced into amphibious battles with them, we need to try to get every man to the shore *alive* to fight. That's why I've been such a fanatic about those landing craft. I see the casualties I saw on the fields in France multiplied if we don't."

"Holland, you remember that Life magazine article about the amphibious tractor that General Little sent, the Alligator? The vehicle that man in Florida invented to rescue hurricane victims? You thought it had possibilities, remember?"

"Yes, you routed it to me. I knew you'd assigned it to General Bradman to investigate. It did look very good to me, but the Equipment Board didn't think much of it when Bradman asked them to check it out. I heard they recommended against trying it. The board said it wasn't armored enough and saw a few other problems. I don't know how they reached their assessment without sending someone to check it out. After the problems we've had getting a chance to try the Eureka, you'll have to forgive me if my confidence in the board is lacking." Smith's voice rose and a frown appeared as he remembered his long battle to test Higgin's boat.

"They did, but Bradman thought it was too good an idea to pass over that quickly. He insisted on getting more detailed information. Some guy named Roebling developed it. When Roebling got Bradman's request, he had an answer back to us in five days, answering all the questions we asked and providing lots more information. He also offered to demonstrate the unit and let us inspect it at any time. Roebling was even willing to pay our expenses to go to Florida. Bradman asked me to approve him sending someone to go take a look at it, which I did. He sent Major John Kaluf down to Clearwater, Florida, to see it." The General purposely waited for Smith to ask for the results.

Holland obliged, "What did Kaluf think?"

"He came back completely sold. Kaluf piloted the unit himself. It operates in surf, deep water, mud morasses, and can smash right through mangroves. Naturally, there are some modifications that would be needed to make it a combat vehicle. But Kaluf believes this is the answer to the landing craft problem when you couple it with Higgins' boat." Holcomb raised his eyebrows. "So do I. Holland, Kaluf shot 400 feet of film of the unit in operation. I'd like you to take a look at it."

"Hell, yes! I'd love to, sir. When can I see the film?"

"Come with me, I've already got the projector set up."

* * *

The corporal running the projector dimmed the lights. The whirr of the projector started and a white tracked vehicle raced down a muddy shore, plowing through small bushes and thick weeds into a marsh, moving swiftly into deeper water then churning along at speed that was reduced, but impressive.

"Damn! Can I see that again?" Smith asked.

"We'll look at it as much as you want," Russell said. "You don't have to see much to understand why Kaluf is excited. But you haven't seen anything yet."

The lights came back on after the fourth time the two Marines watched the film. Holland Smith said, "That unit has tremendous potential. It will revolutionize amphibious warfare. In fact, it will make it possible. Sir, are you considering getting one of these tractors for testing?"

"Holland, I processed the request to the Chief of Naval Operations to purchase one on May 18th."

15

Getting Ready for the Inevitable
1939, Holland Smith
Island of Culebra, the Caribbean

"Deacon, I don't know what we're going to have to do to convince these Navy idiots to scrap all their playing around with those stupid designs the Special Boat Planning Board came up with." Holland Smith pushed his empty plate to the side. He and Colonel William P. "Deacon" Upshur, USMC, sat at the officers mess table discussing FLEX #5, the most recent fleet landing training exercise. "The Higgins boat out-performed everything else we've been experimenting with by such a margin it isn't worth discussing the other designs. We've got nineteen different boats, eighteen of which can't begin to do the job. Either they get hung up on the coral outcroppings, draw too much water to get close enough to land the men, maneuver so poorly they congest the whole beach, or they can't get off the beach after they unload. That's the big one. Most have at least two of those problems." Smith tossed his fork onto the divided metal dish. "They got 1.2 million dollars allocated to design something that's already done for them."

Upshur leaned back in his chair, placing his hands behind his head. He could see Howlin' Mad stoking his boiler as he started to pontificate on his favorite subject: landing craft and the Marines lack of an acceptable unit. "Smitty, you're right, but you're preaching to the wrong congregation." Upshur was in the official capacity as an "umpire" and part of his assigned duties were to report on all facets of the Flex 5 event. "The Higgins boat is what we need, no doubt about it. It would be better if it were longer—like between thirty-five and forty feet. I'm going to say that in my report."

"Uh-huh. You know why we got the boat in thirty foot lengths?" Holland unconsciously balled his hands into fists. "Andrew Higgins told me. He'd suggested they build the boats thirty-nine or forty foot long. The brass said it had to be thirty feet. At first, they wouldn't tell him why; the Navy Special Boat people just said it was a Navy requirement. Well, Higgins is a real fighting Irishman. He kept pushing and pushing. They finally confessed the reason was that ships were already fitted with davits for thirty foot boats. Higgins exploded. He told the bastards, 'To hell with designing a boat to the davits. Why don't you design davits to fit a proper sized boat?' You know what Higgin's doing?"

"No."

"Higgins was so exasperated he went back to New Orleans and has started work on a thirty-six footer. He's building it at his own expense. He tells me he's going to send it to Norfolk when it's complete and insist it's tested."

Upshur chuckled, "No shit! Now there's a man I'd like to get to know. Sounds like he'd be a good recruit for the Corps."

"We need Higgins' Eureka. I've written enough letters to the Marine Equipment Board and Navy Departments from the Special Boat Planning Group and the Bureau of Ships to the Chief of Naval Operations to sink one of those Bureau designed tank lighters. Boy, if that isn't a good example. There hasn't been one successful test of that damned pig boat. One even swamped during a landing in quiet waters. The thing isn't seaworthy and maneuvers like a concrete block."

"I agree with you. That thing ought to be sent to the Dog Patch Navy—you know like in the comic strip. L'il Abner might make good use of it. I know we sure can't. One of the rumors going around Quantico is that the Bureau of Ships has been floating a purchase request for 200 of those things around Corps offices trying to get someone, anyone to sign off on it. They can't even get a private on latrine duty interested. Nobody, and I mean nobody, does anything but cuss it. Word is they allocated a couple million dollars and started work on them without authorization."

Holland raised an eyebrow. "I wonder if the top guys

know about that?"

"Who knows?"

"It makes me boil when I think about being denied enough money to get some Higgins boats and an Alligator or two to try." Smith's face was flushing.

"Alligator? What in hell is an Alligator?" Upshur asked.

"It's the best thing I've seen yet to get troops ashore alive in bad, hostile conditions. It's an amphibious tractor that has tracks like a tank. Holcomb showed me a film of it and he processed a request for one. I understand that his request was denied. The Office of Naval Operations replied that the special boats and lighters had priority over new projects. In other words, we get those useless tank lighters shoved down our throats instead of good equipment like the Eureka and the Alligator."

"It is a shame landing craft are still a big problem. Flex 5 has been a big improvement over Flex 4 as far as our troop training, communications, Navy-Marine coordination, cooperation and improved battle tactics are concerned. Smitty, I know that you continue to be concerned about boat obstacles and reefs, but even the Eureka doesn't solve that problem."

Holland nodded. "Yes, and that's why I'm eager to test out the Alligator. It will crawl right up and over the reefs, crash through barbed wire strung on the beaches, and smash most of the boat obstacles the Japanese are currently using. God, I'm hoping the assholes in the Bureau of Ships don't hold us up on getting approval for that unit like they did on the Higgins Boat."

Upshur looked over Holland's shoulder and held his finger to his lips. "We have company."

Smith turned in his chair to see who was approaching. An ensign he recognized from the ship's communication staff was carrying a large envelope in one hand and was headed straight for them. Holland watched the ensign step up to them, straighten to attention, and salute stiffly.

"Colonel Smith, sir, I have a communiqué for you," the officer announced.

Smith returned the salute, accepted the envelope, and said, "Thank you, ensign." The ensign nodded, executed a smart about face and retreated.

The envelope had no identifying markings other than "Official Marine Corps business, for Colonel Holland M. Smith" typed on its white side. Smith looked at the envelope questioningly. He wasn't expecting anything specific to be sent to him and routine items were supposed to be held in his Washington office.

"Well, aren't you going to open it?" Upshur asked.

Holland lifted his brows and nodded while tearing the envelope open. His eyes scanned the papers inside. He suddenly stopped and reread the papers again.

"Well?" Upshur asked.

"I've been relieved of my duties as Director of Training and Operations and have been assigned to be Assistant to the Commandant of the Corps. I'm to stay here until FLEX 5 is ended. I'm Holcomb's assistant when I return to Washington." Smith said the words with little expressed emotion. It was though someone had suddenly attached a heavy weight to his shoulders.

Upshur observed the change. "Come on, Smitty, this is great for you. It probably means your first star. Think about it. General Holland Smith. It has a good ring to it. I bet you'll have a major troop command in a short time."

"Yes, Deacon, it does sound good. I just want to be worthy of it."

* * *

General Holcomb's office, Washington DC
April 1939

"I don't want to let you down, sir." Smith shook the hand that General Holcomb offered.

"That's the last thing you need to worry about, Holland." The General put a hand on Smith's shoulder. "You've done an outstanding job at every task the Corps has assigned to you. I know you'll do as well on this one."

Holcomb paused, "Just don't get too used to that comfortable desk. You'll be going to the field before long."

"That will be a great honor. I think it's every Marine officer's dream to command a large unit," Smith's comment was an indirect way of getting information he badly wanted.

"That will happen sooner or later." Holcomb smiled. "Probably sooner."

Smith nodded, restraining the grin that tried to invade his face.

"There is one thing I want to mention. I want you to continue your work pointed toward helping us get the landing craft problem solved. The star should help. Looking into *how* to do that is going to be one of your first assignments. That is, how you can do it without crippling the Corps or yourself with the Navy muckity-mucks." A serious expression flitted over Holcomb's countenance, but it quickly reverted to a smile. "We're going to need every good Marine we have to fight the war that's coming. I don't want to lose you in some political snafu."

"I'll do my best to remember that." Smith pinched his lips. "General, how soon do you think it will be before war breaks out? We still aren't ready to fight major amphibious battles with Japan or with any other major power."

"I believe we have time to get ready, but I'm not sure how long. I don't think much will happen until the Soviets decide where they stand. Russia has the largest military in the world. As long as they're a threat to Germany and Japan I don't think you'll see anybody willing to drop the first bomb. If the Russians line up with either the Germans or the Japs, I don't think a full scale war will occur. The British fear the Russians and Communism as much as they do the Germans and the Nazis. They couldn't take them both on. Hitler just took over Czeckoslovakia and his help finished the war in Spain and has set Franco up as dictator. Chamberlain didn't do anything, other than wring his hands. The Versailles Treaty is toilet paper. Hitler's rearmed, quit the League of Nations, annexed Austria with the 'Anschluss,' and taken back Rhineland and Sudetenland. The British and French aren't going to do anything except yell about it. If Hitler was sure about Stalin, he'd be knocking on Paris' door already. I have a contact in the State Department who tells me that we suspect all kinds of intrigues and double deals floating around between all of the European powers. Until Russia chooses sides, I bet nothing major happens. If it does, look out."

"If Russia sides with Britain won't that keep the Japs less aggressive? It seems if the Russians go with the Germans there'll be more cause for concern. Fighting a two front war would be hard even with a military the size the Soviets have. Wouldn't that free up the Japanese to fight us?"

"That's logical, but with the Japs, who knows. They've gotten their political tentacles in Indochina, the Dutch Indies, Thailand, Malaysia, and they're itching to move. I think they believe they can beat us, the British, or the Russians. But I'm betting they don't believe they can beat two of us at the same time. So, as long as the Russians don't choose sides, it will stay peaceful. A disturbed, nervous peace, but no war. Once the Soviets choose a side, things will blow up fast. It will be a year, two at the most, but we'll get drawn into it, just like the last one."

"We've got a lot of preparation and not a lot of time to do it."

"That's what we're counting on you for, Holland, to help get the Marine Corps trained and ready to go."

16

A Young Man's Choice
1940, Ben Bennett
Green Mountain, North Carolina

"Mama, you 'bout ready to eat?" Andrew Bennett called through the front screen door. "I'm hungry 'nough to eat the rear end out of old General Sherman."

"Just a few minutes more, dear," Mrs. Bennett's voice crooned from somewhere in the house. She added a gentle warning, "Please, Andrew, don't talk such on the Lord's day."

Andrew Bennett leaned back in his rocker. He enjoyed his Sunday break from the daily toil required to raise tobacco on his twenty acre farm. One of the simple pleasures he could afford in the hard times the thirties had brought was enjoying sitting on his modest home's front porch. Another was sharing that experience with friends and relatives. Farrell Tipton was one of those friends. The two men watched four of their children, all teenage girls, sit under a huge old hickory tree, chatting and giggling about their favorite subject, boys.

"You all want some ice tea?" Farrell's wife asked from somewhere inside the house. "I'll bring some, if you want."

"Yes'm, I would, thank you kindly," Andrew replied.

Farrell added, "I'll take one, too."

"Farrell, your garden don't look so dry as mine. How you keepin' it watered?" Andrew asked.

"You know that spring up on Collin's place, the one near where I killed that eight point buck last year?"

"Reckon so."

"Well, sir, old Chet and me, we dug it out and put a reservoir there. I furnished the tank and such. We run some garden hose down the mountain to our gardens. We're real careful not to run it out, rain being so scarce." Farrell looked down the steep front yard. A patch of tobacco growing on bottom land near a "branch" suffered in the drought. The tiny stream was reduced to a trickle of water only a few inches wide. "You'uns are powerful dry here."

Andrew nodded. "I thought about damming up the branch, but I ain't got the money to do it right. Besides, it wouldn't do no good 'til next winter. I reckon it wouldn't pond up 'til then. The only spring I got is for house water, so I can't take that. We just need rain. Damn, Farrell, I ain't never seen Jack's Creek so low. Not in forty-two years."

"Yep. If'n it don't rain soon the fish will have to grow legs and learn to eat grass."

The zing of the screened door spring and the clinking ice in glasses announced Brenda Tipton's appearance as she backed through the door opening, iced tea in hand.

"Here you go boys." Her pretty face smiled as she handed them the amber liquid. "Mary Alice says to save your ice for the meal, and Andrew, you need to call Ben for dinner." Brenda disappeared to help Andrew's wife set the table.

"Where's your boy at?" Farrell asked.

"When we got home from church he went down to the vegetable patch across the road. Took his 22. We got a damned ground hog that's ruinin' the potatoes. Between the coons, deer, ground hogs and no rain, I'm wonderin' if'n we'll get a thing out of it." Andrew stood and walked to a wooden pillar supporting the porch roof. He cupped his hand around his mouth and shouted, "Uuuu-Eeee, Ben. Dinner's on."

"You tried fencin' it?" Farrell asked.

"Yep. Don't do no good. The ground hogs dig under it, the deer jump over it and the raccoons climb it. I even tried tying rags and tin cans 'roun—"

The sharp crack of a small caliber rifle interrupted Andrew Bennett's sentence.

Farrell smiled, "I reckon that will do some good."

The four girls had already risen from under the hickory tree and were chattering as they climbed the steep grade to the Bennett house. "They are a growin', ain't they?" Farrell said.

"Yep. Mine are gettin' old enough to have acquired smart mouths. But, I'm workin' on that," Andrew said. He was looking down the rock road that wound around and to the rear of his tobacco shed before it joined the county pavement. As he watched, his son Ben appeared on the road from behind the shed. His 22 dangled from one hand and a large brown furry ground hog hung from its tail, grasped in Ben's other fingers.

"You got him!" Andrew yelled.

Ben raised the varmint up even with his head and called back, "Uuuu-Eeee."

"That young 'un of yours is one fine shot!" Tipton said.

"Yep. Takes after his Grandpa Benjamin, God rest his soul," Andrew said.

Farrell grinned. "Don't it get confusing, always naming your first born son after his grandfather?"

"No. It's a tradition. I reckon Ben's first son will be named Andrew after me. Of course, sooner or later someone will screw it up. Nothing goes on forever."

* * *

Andrew, Farrell and Ben sat around the dining room table as the women and girls whisked the dirty dishes and the meager left-overs to the kitchen.

Farrell rubbed his stomach and said, "Now, that was a mighty fine meal." He looked at Ben and asked, "You're graduating from high school this coming Friday. What you gonna do to help your Pa put food on the table, Ben?"

Ben and his father exchanged knowing glances. Farrell immediately recognized he'd unwittingly stumbled into a contentious subject for the Bennetts.

"I had planned to go to Raleigh, Charlotte, or Knoxville to find work. When I went to Durham for the tryout with Brooklyn, I looked around while I was there, but I couldn't find a job that was any better than here in Burnsville. I haven't heard anything from the Dodgers so I figure I'm not going to be playing baseball."

"I've told him he can stay here and help me with the farm. Maybe find a job close so he can do both. He doesn't like that idea," Andrew Bennett growled. "Life's not good enough here."

"Pa, you know that's not it. I just want to do something different. Since I was seven years old, I've been hoeing tobacco, suckering it, chopping it, drying it and storing it. That's eleven years of tobacco. Hell, Durham is the farthest I've ever been away from here. The only other state I've been in is Tennessee. I want to see the country and maybe the world, places I read about in school. Besides, if I can get a job some place that pays better than around here, I can help you and mom instead of just being another mouth to feed."

"I don't see how you a workin' in one of those there mills in Raleigh or Charlotte is gonna show you the world,"

Ben's father snorted. "There ain't many hula girls a workin' in those places.

Farrell spoke up. "It sounds like you should consider getting in the military. My brother is in the Marines. He's been all over the world. China. Santo Domingo. The Philippines. Honduras. All over. They put clothes on your back and food in your stomach. Pay ain't great, but you don't need much. The bases in the states are real ni—" Farrell saw the look on Andrew Bennett's face and shut up.

"Farrell Tipton, you were in France with me. How in the hell can you even suggest that to the boy?" Andrew's face looked like a thunder cloud. "The Germans and British are at each others throats. France has collapsed—they're out of it. Dunkirk was a bloodbath. The English are hanging on by their fingernails. That new guy they have as Prime Minister, Churchill, is pushing to get us into the war. You think the U.S. won't get involved sooner or later? Bull-shit! I don't want Ben to go through what we did."

"He won't. Remember, The Great War was *the war to end all wars*. The people in Washington say we'll *never* fight in Europe again. Even with what's happening there now, Roosevelt's keeping us neutral. Hell, the British brought this on themselves when they signed that pact with the Poles six days before the Nazis invaded. They knew what was coming. A war like the last one just isn't going to get us involved. Hitler gave England a year to sign a peace treaty before he crushed France, Holland and Belgium. Nah, not us; we aren't getting' into it. Unless we get attacked—how would the Germans do that? Ben might end up in some skirmish in one of the banana republics, that's all." Farrell defended his comments. Life had been better for his Marine brother than it had for him as he scraped and suffered through the depression years.

"What the politicians say in Washington is all bunk. They will lie to you faster than tell you the truth. You got Hitler grabbing everything in Europe and Japan doing the same in Asia. It's just a matter of time till they come for what we got," Andrew said.

"Then *we'll all have to fight anyway, won't we?*" Farrell said.

Andrew Bennett scowled, got up from his chair, and left the room. Farrell and Ben heard the front screened door slam shut.

Ben looked at Farrell for a few seconds before asking, "Would you give me your brother's address? I'd like to write him and ask some questions."

"I'll do better than that. He's coming home on leave in two weeks. I'll see you get a chance to talk to him then."

17

An Extraordinary Machine and Man
1940, Donald Roebling
Roebling's Development Shed, Clearwater, Florida

Brigadier General Emile P. Moses remembered his first visit to Roebling's Clearwater facility. As the auto ferried them to meet Roebling, he'd reread Major Kaluf's report. It was so complementary he'd been suspicious, but cautiously optimistic at what he and his three officer committee would view during their inspection of the new Alligator amphibious vehicle. Toward the end of Kaluf's report he'd reread an underlined passage one last time. It stated:

For the benefit of any officers who have future dealings with Mr. Roebling...it should be explained that the designer, Donald Roebling, and his father, John Roebling, who furnished the necessary funds, are very wealthy people and are not developing this amphibian to make money and cannot be approached on a profit basis. Any additional income would probably be an embarrassment to them. Unlike the ordinary manufacturer who has something he is anxious to sell, they can be appealed to only on the basis of patriotic or humanitarian motives as far as this amphibian is concerned.

General Moses knew John Kaluf to be a man with his feet firmly planted in reality. The Major was not one to use hyperbole or exaggerate in describing situations, things, or people. As the car carrying them to see the vehicle entered Donald Roebling's estate, he could see that Kaluf's comment about the Roeblings being exceedingly wealthy was understated. Moses hoped the description of the machine was as accurate. One of the officers accompanying the General whistled and said, "I forgot to bring my dress blues."

Mindful of Kaluf's comment, Moses had warned, "Gentlemen, be aware that these individuals are very civic minded. They see the development of the unit we're going to look at as a duty. I want all of you to treat our hosts with the utmost respect. When you talk to them, do it like you're in a discussion with the Commandant. Remember, what these people are doing is very important to the Corps." Moses took a deep breath as the car rolled to a stop. Four men approached the car as he'd opened the door. Three were normal height and weight. The fourth was ungainly obese. He knew from talking to Kaluf that man was Donald Roebling.

After seeing the Alligator perform, Moses totally agreed with Kaluf's evaluation and wrote an even more glowing analysis of the amphibian. That report triggered an allocation and approval of $24,500 for a prototype unit's production for the Marine Corps. After a careful study of drawings of the unit and combat conditions it would face, a number of changes were requested. The Roebling's were happy to accommodate the Navy who was purchasing the vehicle.

This time General Moses trip was to conduct a pre-delivery inspection. His intuition told him that neither he nor the Marines would be disappointed. Returning to the Roebling estate with keen anticipation, he would soon see if the eccentric genius had been able to incorporate all or part of the changes that the Corps had requested.

* * *

"I can't express strongly enough how impressed I am with the improvements you've made to your invention, Mr. Roebling. It performs unbelievably well. You and your technicians have done wonders." General Moses wasn't flattering his host. He was truly overwhelmed by what he'd seen during the long day of testing and operation.

"Remember, I'm Donald. Call me Don." Roebling's face beamed at the General's words. "I appreciate your kindness. We have made strides. We've made strides."

"The reports regarding your tractor that Major Kaluf made were outstanding. My initial visit and inspection of the Alligator was impressive. Based on the changes we desired, I'd have been extremely happy if your vehicle would have performed close to the level we requested. But, what you've done—I wish I had some way to do more than express the Marine Corp's sincere gratitude for what you've accomplished. You've far exceeded what we asked for." The General looked at the specification page in his hand, all of which he'd verified during his acceptance inspection. "You increased the water speed to over the 9.5 mph we requested. You increased the land speed to 29 mph. That's far more than we envisioned. It's 1000 pounds lighter than the previous model. You've increased the carrying capacity to 7000 pounds. And, having the cargo area completely flooded with water, and I do mean completely, yet seeing the Alligator still floating and maneuvering, well, it's unbelievable. After seeing your people drive it off a five foot seawall into deep water without capsizing it, I believe it's more seaworthy than any boat I've seen in the same size range. I can't wait until the Marines get the unit!"

John Roebling remained composed, but obviously was pleased with the General's praise. He said, "We thank you, General."

Don Roebling was much more affected by Moses' comments. Though he fought them, tears formed in his eyes. "I thank you, Emile." Donald's voice vibrated as he spoke. "I have some other good news. I've found a local company to help produce the unit if the Marines elect to buy some. It's the Food Machinery and Chemical Company. Some of the parts I couldn't make in my shop were made by them in their Dunedin facility." Roebling took a breath and proudly added, "I didn't need all the money you paid us to do the development work. There is a little more than $4000 left to give back to the government."

Even with his previous knowledge of Don Roebling, the inventor's words caught General Moses off guard. "Don, I'm sure that neither the Corps nor the Federal Government wants you to refund the overage. I'm sure they appreciate your sentiment, but it's not necessary." The general had never heard of anyone wanting to reimburse the government for an over-payment.

"Oh, but I insist! I would feel guilty keeping these funds. When I requested the original amount, I thought the materials would cost more than they did. I won't keep the money. Will you find out who I should return it to?"

Moses squinted at the rotund man whose words left him incredulous. "I'll do my best, Don. Give me a little time on that." He quickly changed the subject. "When do you think we can get the Alligator? Your vehicle has generated a great deal of interest. Our amphibious planning folks are anxious to test it for their purposes. Landing craft have been one of our biggest needs for some time. I'm sure the Alligator is the answer."

"I'll have it in Norfolk for the Navy to test on the 25th of this month." Roebling looked very pleased. "I've already made shipping arrangements. I took the liberty of building some spare parts that we thought you might need. Those were made with a portion of the funds you've already given us. The spares will be sent with the unit. Would you like me to send a couple of my technicians to assist you and the Navy with their tests? Plans have been made. There won't be any cost to the Navy. We'll pay all their expenses."

General Moses sighed and lifted his face. "Mr. Roebling, you are a truly efficient and amazing individual." It was nice to compliment the man without one shred of false flattery being involved.

18

The Irresistible Force meets the Unmovable Object
1941, Holland Smith
Island of Culebra, the Caribbean

"It's the most revolutionary piece of amphibious military machinery ever developed." Captain John Krulak spoke to a steel eyed Admiral who looked over the battleship Texas' rails at an Alligator driving in lazy circles in the blue Caribbean waters. "Ever since General Smith assigned me the task of testing the tractor for combat readiness, I've been more and more impressed on a daily basis. Holland is sold on the unit. It will go anywhere, through anything. I believe it will save untold Marine lives if and when we have to land on a heavily defended beach. The Navy tested the Alligator at Norfolk. We tested it at Quantico. The machine is amazing. General Smith told me to offer you a demonstration, sir."

Admiral Ernest J. King, commander of the Atlantic Fleet, looked at the amphibian dubiously. From the deck of his flagship, the Alligator looked like a cork bobbing up and down in a bathtub. "The damn thing sits awfully low in the water." Leaving the relative comfort of the Texas for a ride in the steel contraption that looked like it was ready to sink at any second wasn't high on his list of priorities.

"Admiral King, the Alligator is very seaworthy. We flooded the whole troop deck and the unit still floated and made headway. I guarantee you won't get any more than a little spray on you." Krulak's weeks of putting the unit through rigorous pounding made him supremely confident in the tractor's capabilities.

The thin, gray haired King glanced down at his immaculate white uniform, then at the young Marine officer. "What do you propose, Captain Krulak?"

"Let me give you a ride from the Texas right up to the palm trees on the beach and then we'll return back here, sir."

King looked at the surf breaking against the coral reef that fronted Culebra. He was in the middle of evaluating reports on FLEX #7 (Fleet Exercise #7). Taking time out of his busy schedule for a joy ride to the beach rankled him. His first thought was to decline Krulak's offer. He looked at the tractor and remembered a discussion he'd had with Holland Smith. It was one of the more pleasant exchanges with the Marine General. One of the few. The relationship between King and Smith during their first joint action hadn't been a smooth one. Both were strong personages with definite ideas about how the landings associated with the mock landings should proceed. King decided he'd make the journey to the beach and back in deference to Smith and inter-service relations, even though he had serious trepidations about the "boat" in which he was about to sail. "Okay, Captain, I'll make the ride to shore with you. How long will the trip take?"

Krulak said, "The round trip won't take more than 45 minutes, sir." Krulak lifted a bull horn he was carrying and called to the circling craft. "Sergeant Draper, please bring the Alligator along side."

* * *

It took Admiral King several minutes to feel comfortable standing on the diminutive deck of LVT-1. The Alligator sat even lower in the water than it appeared from the Texas' rail. It gave King the feeling he had when he was standing in a swimming pool looking outward. Captain Krulak spouted specifications and accolades about the vehicle that churned the water with its "finned" tracks throwing two tails of water out each side of the vehicle's stern. The unit made surprisingly good speed toward the shore. True to the Captain's promise, the tractor shielded its occupants from the spray caused by the amphibian's front plowing through three foot seas. Without vocalizing the fact, King grudgingly admitted that the Alligator was performing much better than he anticipated. Still, the trip interrupted his routine and his work schedule which tried his patience. The best part of the trip would be when it was over. Impatiently, he watched the ocean waves break against the coral reef, begrudging each second as a waste of his time. The tractor gradually approached the reef. With each yard they progressed, the crashing water and foam became more visible. It looked too rough to go over the coral.

Trying not to show his nervousness, the Admiral asked, "Is the surf too high to go into the beach?"

"No. Not at all. We've taken the Alligator over the reef in five to six foot swells. We'll be starting over the coral in a minute. When I say brace yourself, get a good grasp on the side rails, sir." Krulak said.

The tractor was close enough to the coral reef that King could see its shape and color through the gin-clear water. There was only a foot of water covering the shelf that acted as a natural defense for the island. Waves pounded down onto the reef violently. The sergeant driving the unit shouted, "Thirty seconds to go."

"Hang on, Admiral!" Krulak reminded.

King grasped the tractors side with one arm encased in his starched white coat sleeve, resigned to smearing his clean uniform with whatever dirt was present on the amphibian. There was a grinding noise and the Alligator's front end rose abruptly from the ocean, tilting the deck upward at the front by twenty degrees. Within a few seconds, the tractor was on top of the reef, level again, crunching its way over the coral toward the lagoon between the reef and the shore. Sergeant Draper yelled, "Yeee-haww!" as the Alligator successfully crawled onto the reef. Krulak babbled superlatives about the machine's performance as Admiral King regained his dignity and composure.

The tractor lurched forward, crossed reef, and started to slide downward into the lagoon on the shore side of the reef when the whole machine made a violent pitch to the side and a loud twanging noise was accompanied by a string of curse words mumbled by the driver. The unit slid into the shallow water of the lagoon, but forward movement stopped seventy yards from shore. Draper told Krulak, "Captain, I caught the tracks in a crevice on the coral. The track assembly sheared off."

Panic struck Captain Krulak. He yelled to the sergeant, "See if we can make enough headway to get to shore with the one side." Draper frantically operated the controls, but the tractor wallowed sluggishly, but made little progress toward the beach.

"Gentlemen, I'll see you back on the ship." King's words weren't needed to remind the Captain of his presence. As Krulak turned, he saw the angry faced Admiral leaping over the tractor's side into chest deep water. Captain Krulak prudently remained silent as Admiral King waded to shore, his white uniform gleaming under the clear lagoon water.

* * *

The transport ship Harry Lee, off Culebra
late February, 1941

The relationship between Holland Smith and Ernst King during the most pivotal Navy – Marine training operation ever held had remained contentious. Very contentious. FLEX #7 was a great success. But that success had been achieved after a series of battles between the Marine General and Naval Fleet commander. Some of these were due to the inter-service conflict that existed between the Corps and the Navy. Others were products of the two men's personalities who led the exercises. Both were strong willed. Both were intelligent. Both were confident in their abilities. Both were secure in the knowledge of their profession. Both were accustomed to command. Neither was willing to concede to another's point of view if they believed their judgment was correct. It was the first time they'd worked together. Holland Smith believed it would be their last.

The letters that Smith had just finished writing wouldn't help his relationship with the Navy's brass, at least, those connected with the tank lighter program. The boats being purchased to land heavy equipment, such as tanks, were a botched abortive attempt to provide the ships needed. The majority of lower ranking naval officers couldn't believe the Bureau of Ships continued to press for the adoption of the so called "Bureau Boat." In the last few days, Smith had learned that Navy bureaucrats were going ahead with the purchase of ninety-six of the useless vessels. That was $7,000,000 wasted in Holland's eyes. He couldn't sit idly by; he wrote a scathing denunciation letter to the Chief of Naval Operations. His thinly veiled wording came just short of accusing the Bureau of Ships of collusion with manufacturers. Smith thought of the advice that Generals Russell and Holcomb had given him, and the cautions that Ada constantly provided, but his devotion to principle triumphed over self-interest.

Smith firmly believed he'd incurred King's disapproval and that he would be relieved of command in the near future anyway. The running battle the two men fought for the previous ten weeks stemmed from who should be in command of shore operations. King's viewpoint was, since he was in over-all command, he should make the major decisions. Smith believed that once the Marines left the line-of-departure the troops should be under Marine command until the fighting on shore was over. They fought over critical matters such as the selection of landing beaches, the inspection of troops, the sharing of aircraft intelligence photos, and to arguments of less gravity such as, in semantics, the use of the Marine term 'beachhead' versus the Navy term 'beach', and the acknowledgement of receipt of messages which led to a sharp humiliating rebuke administered from King to Smith.

Holland had the utmost respect for the Admiral. King was dynamic, energetic, immensely intelligent, severe and quickly impatient with men who couldn't think as fast as he could. Their conflict arose from the domineering tendencies these virtues produced.

During all these skirmishes, Howlin' Mad refused to give ground when he knew his point of view was correct. King eventually was forced to concede his selection of landing beaches was faulty, and some of his other orders and information incorrect. The Admiral had to rescind his directives, possibly for the first time in his life. In the main, Smith won most of the battles; now he had the feeling he'd lost the war. The fact there wasn't the customary official farewell from King when Smith left the Admiral's flagship after the concluding meeting summarizing the operation reinforced Smith's foreboding.

Even though President Roosevelt had personally authorized Holland's promotion to the rank of Major General during the exercise, Smith's primary reward was the knowledge he'd done an excellent job and the satisfaction and pride coming with that realization. A knock on his cabin door interrupted his introspection.

He opened the door. A neatly dressed ensign waited patiently outside.

The ensign saluted sharply. "General Smith, sir, I have a communication for you delivered by special boat from the Texas and from Admiral Ernst J. King."

Smith took the envelope from the ensign's extended hand. "That will be all, ensign." Holland closed the door believing that the notification of his career's end was lodged in his hand. He returned to his chair, happy that he was in his room's seclusion, for such a blow's gravity would be impossible to conceal from others. Smith exhaled and stared at the envelope for several seconds before tearing the flap open. After pulling out the letter contained inside, he read:

To General Holland M. Smith,

At the close of the recent intensive landing force exercises, I wish to express to you and to the troops under your command in this area, my feeling of satisfaction that such well-trained troops, so well commanded, are an integral part of the Atlantic Fleet, and my confidence in their capacity to do their full part and to do us all credit in whatever active operations may come our way. Well done!

E.J. King

It took several readings and many minutes of contemplation before Holland Smith understood the full meaning of Admiral King's words. It was one of the finest commendations he'd ever received or would ever receive. Smith had learned that, unlike many martinets in high places, Ernie King would say the worst to your face, would never go behind your back, and would reward performance with true generosity. Moreover, it told him he had come in contact with a true rarity; a great leader. Holland wasn't sure, but a feeling in his gut told him his future would be affected by the man he'd recently struggled with and had come to fully respect.

19

Cutting through the Clutter
1941, Don Roebling
Naval Headquarters, Washington, DC

"How much longer will it be?" Donald Roebling asked.

"It shouldn't be much longer." An immaculately dressed enlisted man sat behind his desk as though it was a fortress, clearly dismissing his visitor's question.

"Could you check?"

"Uh-huh. In a few minutes."

Roebling's eyes would have liked to have burned holes through the unsuspecting clerk. Don was frustrated. And damned angry. Sitting in a waiting room in Washington was the last place he needed to be. He was trying his best to do what he believed he should as a good American. It seemed as though the people who should have been helping most were more interested in paperwork and politics than accomplishing what his Marine Corps contacts told him would be needed *soon!*

Over the last year, Roebling watched the world situation go from bad to chaotically dire. England was hanging on to its existence by its fingernails. Goering and his Luftwaffe were doing their best to bomb the British to their knees. Most of Great Britain's war equipment was left on the European continent after the evacuation at Dunkirk. Their moat, the English Channel, was all that protected them from total defeat. The British Navy was the one major element left in its defense structure that the Nazis could not easily crush. The indomitable spirit of the British people kept the flame of victory alive though it flickered and struggled in the winds blowing against them.

More and more countries were drawn into the conflict. It seemed that the only part of the world that wouldn't be eminently consumed by the war's fires was the western hemisphere. The race to massive death accelerated by huge steps when Hitler broke his treaty with Stalin and invaded the Soviet Union. The destruction and human carnage grew at a dizzying pace in those early months of the war between the two most powerful armies in the world. In that conflict's early stages, German technology and military leadership extracted a fearful toll on the Soviets who depended on the sheer weight of numbers to wage war. Roebling read newspaper accounts of tragedies blotting out human life literally by the hundreds of thousands. The toll reported for the Russian Army dead, in Ukraine alone, was estimated to be over 200,000 in the current month. The loss of civilian life was even more appalling. Though he had no way of knowing, they drastically understated the cataclysm.

Roebling couldn't understand how many Americans could blithely dismiss the carnage in Europe. There were those who felt no sense of concern. True, war in the Western Hemisphere wasn't close, but the Nazis had strong influence in Latin American countries like Argentina. Unchecked, the disease would surely spread and there was no guarantee the Atlantic Ocean would provide a barrier. Worse, some individuals in the US military *he dealt with* felt no sense of urgency. These bureaucrats could see no need to personally involve or inconvenience themselves. What was true in the general population was, astonishingly, true in the US government.

"You," Roebling read the man's desk name plate, "Corporal Carter, check with that fellow Clinton. Now!"

The clerk exhaled disgustedly, nodded and picked up his phone.

Despicable, Roebling thought. He wished he could fire the man before he went back to his business. Good God! The events of the last sixty days made things so clear to Donald he wondered how anyone could *not* see war was racing toward America. Roosevelt had frozen all German and Italian assets in America in mid-June, followed by the same action against the Japanese in late July. Most recently, he had suspended all export of oil to "aggressor" nations. How much plainer could it be? Roosevelt was pursuing a course that would inevitably lead the U.S. into war.

We were already involved with Lend/Lease, a program that furnished weapons to the British for the right to place our troops in English western hemisphere bases which they could no longer defend. American volunteer pilots fought the Japanese Air Force in China and the United States was furnishing various kinds of assistance to the fragmented Chinese governments. American ships and sailors were serving, and dying, in convoys escorting merchant vessels not flying the U.S. flag on their way to the beleaguered British Isles. The United States was neutral by pronouncement only.

Most of his associates in the Marines and Navy saw the tempest coming and were racing to get ready. In the majority of U.S. military personnel's minds, the rest of the country wasn't. Roebling did his part by struggling to make the Alligator a functional part of the Marines' arsenal. Donald spent non-stop days and nights producing the tractor drawings from his and his men's minds, the only places the information resided. When a government legal expert showed concern about multiple people manufacturing patented items used in the Alligator, Roebling simply signed over his patents to the government without asking a cent for them. When the Marines needed a quick engineering change, and they had asked for many, he had the work done within days of the request When the Marines wanted the vehicle to do something more or different, Roebling volunteered his time, designing and building the improvement while steadfastly refusing any compensation. After many delays, the Navy finally purchased more prototypes. He and his men put their heart and soul into producing these test tractors the Marines begged for, production that took less time than the approval from governmental bureaucrats who moved maddeningly slow.

He was about to meet another individual he feared would be just one more disappointment in what Roebling considered a bottomless pit of incompetence. The order for 200 of the LVT-1, the model designation the Marines and Navy assigned to the Alligator, were starting to be manufactured. Donald was in the naval offices to expedite approval for building a facility in Lakeland, Florida, with the company Roebling chose as a partner, a partner needed to be able to produce the sized orders contemplated. Massive production was impossible for his small shop. The Marines anticipated that large quantities of Alligators would be required to fight an amphibious war in the Pacific. But needed approvals were painfully slow traveling on the paper train that was official Washington.

"Mr. Roebling." A lieutenant commander stood behind Don. Roebling hadn't noticed the thin young man's approach.

"Yes?" A four-hour wait hadn't improved Roebling's disposition.

"I'm Chuck Clinton. I'm with the procurement office. I'll be handling the coordination on your order from now on." The officer had the phony smile pasted on his face that Don recognized as a standard part of official Washington's uniform.

"Good. I know who you are and what you do. Is the land purchase approval ready?' Don wasn't in the mood for pleasantries.

"Well, I've good news. The basic approval for the company, Food Machinery and Chemical, has been made."

"Then we can go ahead and start the buildings?" Roebling heard the double speak to which he had become accustomed over the last two years.

"Almost. The Navy has a question about the location."

"Now what?" Roebling would have liked to strangle the smooth talking officer. "You people said you wanted a location on a lake and marsh so the vehicles could be tested. You wanted a place on the railroad. You wanted a place away from the coast to keep it from being shelled. You wanted a place where it could be constructed rapidly. The Lakeland site is all those things. What's wrong with the location?" Don's patience was exhausted.

"It's the road." Clinton whined.

"Yeah, it has a road to it—how do you expect people to get to and from work?" Roebling was getting loud. Other people's heads in the waiting room swiveled to watch the circus that had suddenly arrived at the Navy offices. "They don't have wings to fly in! What shit is this?"

Clinton looked shocked, "Mr. Roebling, I can assure you—"

"You can't assure me of anything! What exactly is the problem?" Roebling was only a half octave short of screaming.

"Some of the staff feels, because the road is paved and it runs between the plant site and the lake, the tractor's tracks might tear up the pavement when you test the vehicle and that could upset the local town's people." The Lieutenant Commander looked about him as he spoke, possibly marking an exit if escape were to become necessary.

Roebling struggled up from the two chairs he was sitting on. "Listen to me. You go back and tell "some," whoever that is, I'm going to buy the property and build that plant myself if you haven't got anybody in the administrative office with brains enough to do it. Before I leave here, I'm going to see Holcomb, King, and Knox, and if I have to, Roosevelt. I had to go to Congress to give back the $4,000 you people wouldn't take, so you should know I do what I say I'm going to do. Which way is Secretary Knox's office?"

Fear showed in Clinton's face. "Now, Mr. Roebling, we don't want you to get upset. We're just doing our jobs."

"No, you're not! I'm doing it for you. I'm going to do

what is right for this country; you should start to do the same." Roebling shook his fat finger in the officer's face. "I'm going to see that the plant gets started. Now, tell me where Knox's office is. Or Holcomb's. Or King's. I *know* how to get to see Roosevelt."

Clinton lowered his voice, "Sir, let me take this back to my superior for a few minutes." The lieutenant commander quickly left the room.

An hour later Roebling left with full approval to proceed with the plant's construction. When Don Roebling set out to accomplish something, it got done, whether it was designing a revolutionary piece of equipment or humbling bureaucrats.

20

Leading the "Leader"
1942, Andrew Higgins
The White House, Washington, DC

"Ah, Andrew, come in, come in." Seated in his office, Franklin D. Roosevelt warmly welcomed a friend of his and of the country he governed.

Andrew Higgins returned Roosevelt's smile, "Hello, Mr. President."

"Sit down. How are things down in New Orleans?" Roosevelt's greeting was genuine. He liked and respected the big Irishman who was one of the banes of Navy, Army, and Federal bureaucrats who cringed at the mention of his name. He'd never known Higgins to mislead him or any government official, a rarity in the many persons he dealt with.

"Very well, Mr. President." Higgins slid into a chair across from the huge, highly-polished wooden desk that served as Roosevelt's home base. "I wanted to stop by and give you an update on how the production is going on the LCVPs, the LCIs and LCTs. My sources in the Navy and Marines tell me we're close to using them extensively in the Pacific for the first time. You keep a close watch on what the services need, so I thought you'd be interested."

"I certainly am. Your sources keep you well informed. Sometimes, I think you know more about what's going on in the War Department than my generals and admirals do." Roosevelt leaned forward to make his point. "We are going to start our first permanent offensive moves against the Japs. It's scheduled soon, very soon. Naturally, I can't tell you where. Your equipment figures prominently in future operations. We are planning a series of these actions as soon as our resources in the Pacific are sufficient. Your craft, combined with the amphibious tractors, will be critical to the success of our plans. The European theater, helping re-arm Britain and Russia, and getting ready for operation Torch—sorry I can't tell you about that—are consuming the bulk of our material and efforts. That includes your boats."

"After Torch, it might be a little while until you need more of my stuff in Europe."

"You know about Torch?" Roosevelt looked and sounded concerned.

"Just that it's planned for late this year and will be in Europe or Africa. No specifics. Your Army and Navy people have to tell me a little to guide my scheduling." Higgins felt it was wise not to reveal how much he'd heard about the invasion of North Africa.

The president relaxed a little.

"Oh, I have heard they're being lent to the Brits for some raids in Norway and on the French coastline."

Roosevelt leaned back and took a puff of the cigarette held in his cigarette holder. He looked at Higgins, raising both eyebrows. "Don't tell me you have connections at the British Admiralty, too."

"No, sir, I don't. Just a guess from shipping instructions." Higgins chuckled. "If you have someone I can bug about buying my boats over there, give me their names."

Roosevelt roared with laughter. "The next time I see Churchill, I'll get you those names. Maybe you'll split your time between London and Washington. Then, hopefully, I can get rest from the administrative people and other idiots that are always complaining to me about you interfering with their jobs." The President took another drag on his cigarette and narrowed his eyes. "Seriously, Andrew, we have been talking about a time table to go back to the continent. Winston and I have somewhat of a disagreement on the scheduling; I'm a little more impatient than he. But when it does happen, your boats are going to be the cornerstone of what we're planning."

"We'll be able to supply you with whatever you need, when you need it." Higgins tilted his head to the side. "The LCVP orders are well ahead of schedule. The design for that unit is fairly stable, so I've decided to produce a small additional quantity for emergencies and for future orders while the line is set up. We're slightly ahead on the LCIs, but we have lots of changes that we're incorporating in them. That's slowed us a little. The LCTs are on schedule, but that might change. The Marines down at New River and in the Solomon Islands tell us that they might need some LCT changes to accommodate the new Sherman tanks. Once we settle on what has to be done, I don't see why we can't get back on, or ahead of, schedule quickly."

"That's certainly reassuring. So many of our suppliers spend time telling us why they can't make schedule and how impossible their task is. It's refreshing to hear from someone *who... just... does... the job.*" Roosevelt slipped into his politician's role as he adopted an overly warm, but serious expression to accompany his words. "Andrew, the U.S. government, the military, the American people, and I, all owe you a debt of gratitude. Individuals like you and that Roebling fellow assure me we will win this war. We need every good man we can find in or out of the military. You have my sincere thanks." Roosevelt smiled paternally.

"I hope you're serious about needing every good man. In fact, that's the primary reason I've come to visit you today." Higgins leaned forward in his chair as he prepared to press the President for what would be an unspoken, but asked for favor. Andrew's features became sharp, his eyes intense. "I'd like to know what's happening to General Howlin' Mad Smith?"

Roosevelt's demeanor changed immediately. His posture and face reflected his dislike for the conversation's change. "He's doing well as far as I know," Roosevelt said coldly.

"That's not my understanding, Mr. President. You just told me that we need every good man we can get, in or out of the military. Well, Howlin' Mad is a very, very, very good man. One I think we can ill afford to cast aside on a pretext."

"This is *not* business about boats." The President became huffy and swelled like a toad defending itself.

"No, it's not about boats; it *is* about winning the war." Higgins placed his hands on the desk and leaned forward over its edge. "That's what we all want. The bunk about him being too sick for strenuous duty is bull-shit and you know it. That man is in better shape than most forty year olds."

"Andrew, he's been diagnosed with diabetes," Roosevelt countered.

"Diabetes, my foot. He hasn't the first symptom of diabetes. I know he's had two subsequent blood tests and both came up negative. A directive suddenly appears to test all officers at sixty and he's practically first in line, it seems peculiar to me. I know Smith isn't the easiest person to get along with. That nickname of his is well deserved. But he knows more about amphibious warfare than any other admiral or general I've met by twice. What's more, most of them acknowledge that fact. When Holland sees something that needs to be done, he gets it done and worries about consequences and politics later. Many of the fore-flushing admirals and generals I've come in contact with are too interested in seeing the right political thing is taken care of, not the job. Most of them have lost focus on what their responsibilities are."

Roosevelt stared at Higgins, "We all have to look after our own responsibilities. I understand that Smith's problem is that he gets involved with *others'* business too much."

Whether real or imagined, Higgins bristled at what he saw as a veiled mild threat. He paused, carefully wording his next comments, both to defend his friend Holland and to express his total lack of intimidation. Andrew pressed even farther forward. "Franklin, the reason I'm building boats for you and the government today is a result of Smith's persistence. The boats you just said are so important. Howlin' Mad's had to force others to do their job so he could do his. I've never known him to be self-serving when he raises an issue. Can you say the same for the people who are his detractors?" Higgins paused to allow the President to speak. Roosevelt remained stone-faced and silent. Andrew continued, "He's a perfectionist. He expects perfection of himself. He expects perfection of those he works with. I can think of far worse things to be when the lives of thousands of men and the outcome of battles depends on a man's actions. He's not afraid to take responsibility for his decisions or defend them; that's another good trait."

Roosevelt seemed to soften a little. "Holland Smith is an excellent man and general, there's little disagreement over that."

Higgins leaned back, lowering his intensity as the President lowered his. "You said you were concerned that Holland was afflicted with an ailment. I think some folks believe he is. It's an ailment you and I wouldn't see as such, but some governmental officials might. He suffers from honesty." Andrew saw Roosevelt's face begin to cloud. Higgins quickly raised his hand and said, "I'm not accusing anyone of dishonesty, I'm just defending Smith's. I think his problems go back to the Truman Commission and the hearings that were held. They are a big part of the reason I'm making the tank lighters today."

Roosevelt looked at him questioningly, "What do you mean? General Smith didn't testify at those hearings as I recollect. Why would those impact Smith? Actually, the hearings did uncover the Bureau purchased a craft design for the lighters which wasn't suitable and eventually they corrected the problem by using your boat designs. Smith should have liked that."

"You're right, Smith didn't *testify* at those hearings. He

was asked to, but declined. He knew enough to realize he'd be in an untenable position. Remember Taussig? What you may not know is that the letters he'd written to the Chief of Naval Operations regarding the tank lighters poor perform-ance and the Bureau of Ships inefficiency were some of the prime documents used in the committee's investigation. Smith told the lawyer for the committee he'd said every-thing he had to say in that correspondence. Look at the re-sults, 1100 units the military didn't want; seven million in wasted dollars that the armed forces desperately needed. You know the cloud that came down on everyone associ-ated with that mess and the changes that resulted. Many of those bureaucrats blame their problems on Holland, others too, but definitely Smith. Personally, I can't understand why most of those folks are still around. Even if there isn't any corruption involved, they'd at least be guilty of horrible judgment."

Roosevelt nodded his head. "I would have to agree with your last statement." There was an enlightenment to facts not known in the president's eyes which he took pains to conceal, but Higgins knew things were about to change for his friend General Smith.

"I admit readily that Howlin' Mad was very important in getting me a chance to show what my Eureka boat could do. He championed it to be the backbone of our amphibious operations, that's true. I like him. But that doesn't impact my judgment regarding his competency as a fighting general. I know he wants to lead the men he's been training for the last two years. Mr. President, I believe there's a need for his leadership. I don't want his services lost because of politics." Higgins leaned far back in his chair. He felt he'd done his best for his friend.

Roosevelt remained silent, his face becoming an inscrutable mask. "Andrew, I'm sure that General Smith will have his opportunity when the time and his superiors feel it is right. In fact, I can assure you of that." The President paused for several seconds, but Higgins knew when to remain silent. "You, being his friend, might consider advising him, that though it is sometimes unwanted and distasteful, politics are often involved and are unavoidable. He should keep that in mind. Focusing on what concerns us most is the key thing, wouldn't you agree?"

"Yes, Mr. President, I do." Higgins understood what Roosevelt had really said.

"Tell me, Andrew, how is that wonderful wife of yours?"

21

An Old Man Gets His Chance
1943, Holland Smith
Naval offices, San Francisco

"The way you folks have described the operation at Attu makes me think of a Texas barbeque where the host forgot to kill the meat. You men had the enemy on the spit, beat the pants off him and right when he should have surrendered, he staged that suicide attack. It's certainly sobering to realize the Japs reacted that way to getting whipped." There was a unique atmosphere in any meeting Fleet Admiral Chester Nimitz ran. Interjecting his early life experiences in Texas with its western, low key, informal nature, helped calm the most explosive situations and added levity to gatherings that were often contentious. This cordial meeting was held to discuss the aftermath of the Aleutian campaign's first segment.

Seated around the table were some of the individuals who would prove the most crucial to America's Pacific victory. Besides Nimitz, Admiral Ernst J King, now chief of Naval Operations, Rear Admiral Francis W. Rockwell, commander of the amphibious forces at Attu, Major General Holland Smith, who trained the troops that made the landing, and US Army Major General Albert E Brown, the ground commander, assessed the attack and defeat of the Japanese on Attu.

"We've discussed the action in detail. The Japanese are well trained. They're a tough opponent. We knew that from Guadalcanal and the Solomons. I want to know what the two most important things each of you learned as a result of the Attu battle—that doesn't have to do with the Jap's capabilities." King was impatient, as always. He fidgeted, chaffing at Nimitz's relaxed manner of conducting the meeting. "Let's get to it. Francis, you start."

"The most important thing I learned was that we need to improve our intelligence effort significantly if we want to streamline our operations and keep them from being costly." Rockwell was a veteran officer, had been in the Philippines when Japan invaded there and was evacuated with MacArthur when he was sent to Australia. He understood amphibious warfare better than most in the Navy and Smith enjoyed a good relationship with him. "Let me give you some examples. The soil conditions ashore were unexpected. Tundra is soft and spongy. Heavy equipment that we managed to land was practically useless. It bogged down and sat in the way in many cases. We didn't know where the roads were and which ones were usable for us to move supplies. Maps we had were useless. The LVT-1 was what saved us. We need to plan for more of those. In bad road conditions like we experienced they made a huge difference. Those Alligators are great ammunition and supply carriers as well as amphibious craft." Rodkwell paused. "But, what I'd consider the biggest failing was the lack of knowledge about the enemy. We didn't have an accurate count of Jap soldier strength nor where the Japs had guns emplaced or strong points set-up. Our naval shelling was ineffective because much of what we targeted were storage sheds and rock formations. The Japanese use camouflage to good effect, so I know it's not easy. Luckily, there were far less enemy troops on Attu than we thought. Our aerial reconnaissance must be upgraded significantly and we need to interview local residents or individuals who have knowledge of the terrain to ease our operation."

King nodded, making a few notes as Rockwell spoke. "What else?"

"We need to be sure we have transports in adequate numbers to transport the equipment and supplies needed in an amphibious landing like this one. We didn't have half enough. If there had been more Jap troops on Attu, or the beaches more heavily defended, we'd have had trouble keeping up with our logistical needs. There would have been critical shortages of many things. And what gets shipped and how it's stored on those transports is critical. Somehow we got musical instruments in the first deliveries to the beach when we needed ammunition."

"That's not good." Nimitz shook his head. "I thought we had loading and landing priorities straightened out."

"I think we do under normal circumstances, but the lack of ships caused confusion and some unsound decisions." Rockwell said.

"We'll look at both items," King growled, "but remember, there are going to be times when conditions aren't ideal and you have to make do with a few less transports than you need." He looked at General Brown. "How about you, Al? What would you recommend?"

"We needed to assemble more strength in some locations before we started offensive action. That would reduce our casualties. It wasn't possible to do that because of supply movement problems. I agree with Rocky. Some more of those LVTs would have been helpful. Those tracked vehicles could have operated where our wheeled trucks weren't worth much. Our equipment needs to be more suitable for the weather conditions we're facing. That's important. Our men had trouble adapting to the differences in tactics we were taught for the landing, versus those the Army normally use. A longer training period for the men should solve that. And, I believe this is an important point, the training needs to be in the same environment they'll face during battle. Our men had to adapt to the weather conditions and the terrain as well as fighting the enemy. Training in a place like Attu would have been a great help."

"Okay, General," Nimitz said. "The training is a must. I think it would be a good idea to make some of the LVTs available for shuttling supplies from the beach to the front."

King grunted his agreement. "How about you, Holland?"

"We definitely need those LVTs and we need more accurate pre-landing bombardment."

King looked at Holland, "What else? Those have been mentioned. Anything tactical?"

"The two most important things I think we can do are to be sure we move off the beach faster and increase our training for the suicide attack our boys faced at the battle's end. First, the longer our men take to organize and get their equipment assembled to begin their attacks, the greater the chance they'll get pulverized as they sit on the beach. Concentrations of troops like those we had on Attu's beaches in the landing's early stages invite their destruction. That's an artillery man's dream. We need more training, as Albert suggested, and we need to streamline the material we need to fight with on the beachhead. There's a big difference between Army and Marine tactics and we need to see they're reconciled when we're attacking together. Though no Marines were involved, this was evident at Attu. Second, and I think this is the most important problem to correct, the Banzai attack the Japanese used has to be accounted for in our training and in our combat readiness. This is different than what we've seen on Guadalcanal and other places in the South Pacific. There was no real military objective on Attu. Those Japanese simply tried to kill as many of us as they could *and* to get themselves' killed. Those men and officers knew they weren't going to be rescued by the Jap fleet. Normally, that would call for surrender. I have to believe that the actions of the Japanese were planned and part of their doctrine, not just an individual action. We had many of our wounded slaughtered in hospital tents because we didn't expect a suicide charge. I'm going to train our men to expect a last-ditch suicidal attack when the Japs have lost the battle."

"That's good, and something we can take action on. Anything else, Holland?" King asked.

"Just that what Rocky and Al said about logistics is very important. I'd suggest that we use the LVTs for supply delivery to the lines in bad terrain, after the beachhead is secured. We can have the Higgins LCT and LCI boats and the DUKWs take over ship to shore unloading duty. The LVTs were used extensively as carriers at Guadalcanal and in the Solomons and performed excellently."

"Makes sense." King looked around the table and said, "Anything else, gentlemen?" The men remained silent. "Alright, let's get back to the war."

As the men filed out of the room, Nimitz approached Holland Smith. "Holland, I'll be down in San Diego for the next week or two. Let's try to get together while I'm there. My wife's with me, maybe we can all have a meal before I go back to Pearl."

"Fine, Admiral, I'm sure something can be arranged." Holland left not knowing if Nimitz's interest was a good or bad omen.

* * *

Holland Smith's back yard, San Diego, CA
June 1943

"Even if you don't get the chance to command the troops you trained, Holland, the success they're having in the Pacific goes back to what you instilled in them at New River, Solomon Island and Camp Elliot over the last three years." Ada Smith tried vainly to raise her husband's spirits. "You're contributing to the war effort just as much as if you were out in the South Pacific."

Smith took a deep breath. "It's not the same, dear. When you train men, you feel responsible for them . . . the way they perform, their safety *and* how they're treated before and after battle."

"You were able to see the results of your training efforts at Attu, Holland. Wasn't it gratifying for you to see those men perform so well and fight to a victory?" Ada walked behind the chair Holland sat in and put her hands on his shoulder. "Sugar, you've done a wonderful job for the Marines and the Army."

"But I can do so much more. I should be in the Pacific planning operations, seeing the battles through and protecting the Marines from bad treatment." Holland shook his head. "To be shuttled aside because I did what was right for the Marines and the country is so unfair. The reason I'm not in the Solomons today is because I fought the Navy brass and the Bureau of Ships. I was the one who let the cat out of the bag and wouldn't stay quiet. We wouldn't have the Higgins boat today or the LVT so quickly if I hadn't pushed hard."

Ada rubbed his shoulders. After a few silent moments she asked, "Holland, if you were given the same situation today; if you saw mistakes being made in the Navy or Marine upper echelons, would you sit by silently or would you fight what you thought was wrong, regardless of the personal consequences?"

"I'd fight without question."

"Then, dear, maybe you'll have to learn to be satisfied and proud of the accomplishments that you've already made. Be happy you maintained your values and forget what you might have done if you were less of a man." She turned her husband's face around so she could look into his eyes. "I know you'll be disappointed that you aren't a Napoleon, a Jackson or a Lee. But, Honey, if you don't get the opportunity to fight the Japanese it won't make you any less valuable to the Corps or less of a military leader. Besides, I have this feeling Nimitz will ask you to serve with him. He's too sharp a judge of talent to let you sit idle if he needs you. You've always told me that his strength is selecting good people to work for him. When you meet with him next week, maybe he'll ask you to join his staff."

"Ada, I sincerely hope you're right."

"Oh, I am. Though you don't always remember it, I know you're quite a man."

* * *

In a Coronado flying boat, mid-Pacific
July, 1943

The South Pacific's ever-present thick clouds hovered around Admiral Nimitz's personal Coronado aircraft as he flew back to Pearl Harbor. Those puffs of vapor produced a gloomy atmosphere, one appropriate for Holland Smith who sat in a seat next to a window. He watched the heavy chiseled banks of moisture float by; clouds that shrouded islands and brought torrents of rain that made fighting in the South Pacific hell. Howlin' Mad's attention wasn't on the cumulus formations outside the plane. He was becoming increasingly depressed. Nimitz's invitation to Smith to accompany him on a combination planning and troop inspection tour of the South Pacific area had sharply raised Holland's hopes for a field command, the goal he saw as his career's culmination.

The trip started very positively. He had an opportunity to meet with Nimitz's staff in Hawaii; in some cases Smith renewed old relationships and in others he established new ones. At various times during the sojourn, he'd met with Admirals Raymond Spruance, Bill "Bull" Halsey, and the irascible Kelly "Terrible" Turner. At that time, they represented the most prominent U.S. Navy leadership in the Pacific Ocean area. They would remain so for the entire war.

Nimitz visited bases at Suva in Fiji, Noumea in French New Caledonia, Espiritu Santo in the New Hebrides, and Guadalcanal. Sitting in planning meetings for the upcoming assault on New Georgia had been fascinating and had encouraged Smith. Before the meeting, a rumor circulated that Nimitz and Halsey were considering changing the Marine command in the South Pacific. Naturally, Holland hoped he'd receive it. Nimitz remained silent. But it was after his trip to Guadalcanal that Smith's morale twisted into knots.

Smith visited that island's battlefields. It had special meaning for him. He'd trained the men who had fought and died there. A visit to the graveyard disclosed familiar names. It was stirring because the amphibious doctrine Howlin' Mad had help father was partially proven sound on that remote South Pacific Island. Pride at having taught that incredible body of men, who fought brilliantly and, though inadequately equipped, achieved victory by exhibiting the willingness to fight and die fighting. On the heels of that pride was what Smith saw as the increasingly depressing probability he'd never get the opportunity to command his troops in battle. He sat on the plane returning him to Honolulu in as gloomy a state as the weather outside the Coronado's window. He believed he'd been robbed of the honor of leading his Marines in their first battles and now would be denied any chance of field command.

A hand on his shoulder shook him from his melancholy. "General Smith, Admiral Nimitz would like you to join him up forward in the cabin." The young lieutenant commander stood by respectfully as Smith slid from his seat and stepped forward to sit next to the Admiral.

"You wanted to see me, Chet?"

Nimitz put down the magazine he'd been reading and looked at Smith seriously. He clasped his hands together and said gravely, "Holland, I am going to bring you out to the Pacific this fall. You will command all Marines in the Central Pacific area. I think you will find your new job very interesting."

* * *

Later as the plane touched down in Pearl Harbor, Smith repeated, "Thank you for the opportunity, Admiral."

"Don't be in a rush to do that. We're going to activate a modification of the Orange Plan I know you're familiar with. It isn't going to be easy. By far, the toughest fighting the Marines will see is ahead, but I'm sure you're the right man for the job."

Holland Smith knew he was.

22

"No Vehicles, No Invasion."
1943, Holland Smith
Kelly Turner's office, Pearl Harbor, Hawaii

Not all battles are in fields, in hills, on beaches, or on the sea. Nor are all battles waged by enemies. The one occurring in the naval conference room at Pearl Harbor was one that continued day after day as the principals involved in the planning and command of the Gilbert Islands assault, operation GALVANIC, struggled with each other. The individuals leading the two sides were Admiral Richmond Kelly Turner and Holland McTyerie Smith. Two harder, more stubborn men have seldom been called on to function as a team. Their nicknames, "Howlin' Mad" Smith and "Terrible Turner" truly represented their temperaments. However, this marriage made in hell, created by Admiral Nimitz, doomed the Japanese in the Central Pacific. The two perfectionists' joint waging of the war across that vast ocean was unparalleled because of the unbelievable difficulty of assaulting heavily defended beaches and the success they achieved.

Nimitz realized the problems that might evolve when he selected the angry warriors to seize Japanese held islands on the way to Tokyo. He surmised that Turner and Smith would claw at each other like two male cats fighting for a lady, but put aside differences and jealousies when the operations started. Nimitz surmised correctly. He knew they were the best men for the jobs he had to get done. Placing them under the direct command of studious, analytical, and calm, Admiral Raymond Spruance, provided them a referee when impasses were reached. While the Fifth Fleet command chain placed Holland Smith reporting directly to Kelly Turner, Nimitz and Spruance wisely defined Smith and Turners' roles very clearly. This proved to be pivotal; the major problem between the two assault force commanders revolved around what the boundaries of each others authority was. Early in the planning of GALVANIC it became necessary for Spruance to draw a primary line of command. His line was simple—the invasion was under Navy control until the assault troops started for the beaches—then the Marines commanded. Though this solved most issues, Smith and Turner, both pugnacious leaders, nibbled at the edges of their assigned roles like boxers circling the ring.

GALVANIC was the first assault of its type in the Pacific. The bitter fighting at Guadalcanal and other places in the Solomons was of a different nature. Landings there were either against light opposition or sites that lacked the prepared positions the Marines would face in the Central

Pacific. The Solomons battles were fought *after* the landings on larger densely forested jungle islands, often in brutal, desperate *small unit actions.* The Gilberts, Marshals, Carolines, Mariannas, Palaus, and Iwo Jima were completely different. These objectives were often tiny islands covered with a multitude of camouflaged, reinforced and fixed gun emplacements that barred the Marines way. Victory through maneuver in the restricted space the small islands provided was impossible just as Pete Ellis had envisioned in the '20's. Defeating the Japanese meant one thing, frontal assaults. The Marines had no alternative to the deadly, vicious, carnage filled attacks on these tiny bits of coral, sand, jungle, and, sometimes, volcano formed hills.

Those that go first are pioneers, and, as the saying enlightens, "You can tell pioneers by the arrows sticking in their asses." GALVANIC was no exception. Further vindication of Nimitz's judgment in selecting the Turner/Smith team was that they learned from the mistakes made in GALVANIC, corrected them and improved on those things done correctly. Those mistakes were costly in the most precious of currencies, human lives. That cost would modify Navy plans as it charged across the Pacific to Tokyo's doorstep. In fact, those changes started prior to GALVANIC's first shot being fired.

"I don't like it. This is going to cost Marine lives and

after we take the island, if we can, what's the benefit?" Smith viewed the map lying on the conference table depicting Nauru Island. Reconnaissance photos littered the table, covering parts of the map. Mixed among the photos were intelligence reports from various sources such as descriptions of the island made by former residents. Smith looked up at Kelly Turner.

Turner glanced at the map. "Captain Theiss, if we take Nauru, are we going to be in range of Jap aircraft based in the Marshals?" He looked at his chief of staff, his eyes burning with the intensity that always shone there, the pupils being pinpoints of fire peeking out from under bushy salt and pepper eyebrows.

"Yes," was the Captain's simple answer.

"Then why in hell are we wasting time considering Nauru?" Turner growled.

Colonel Erskine, Smith's chief of staff volunteered, "We need to have something to tell the Joint Chiefs of Staff (JCS). They're the ones that came up with this nightmare."

"We're not doing this," Turner said.

"Yes. *I* agree we should reject Nauru as part of GALVANIC." Smith tacitly reminded Turner his wasn't the only voice that counted at the table. Both Turner and Smith's staffs looked at "Terrible Turner" to see how he'd react.

Turner frowned, "I'm glad *you* agree." He tried to keep

his displeasure out of his tone.

"Then, let's draft a letter to the JCS," Theiss recommended, deftly changing the issue.

"We're going to have to recommend an alternative to Nauru. Do any of you have a suggestion?" Smith stared at members of his staff.

"How about Makin?" Lieutenant Colonel Hogaboom recommended. "We know that island from previous action there, it's out of range of land-based aircraft in the Marshals, there aren't as many defenders garrisoned on it, it's on the transit line from here and intelligence doesn't show intensive defense positions built on it."

"Good suggestion." Holland nodded and pointed to the map. "Tarawa is going to be bad. We don't need two blood baths. It will increase the size of our troop reserve because we won't need as many to assault the beaches at Makin."

"That means we won't have to use as many transports. There won't be as much distance between the two supporting task forces for the fleet to worry about and Makin is a lot farther from Truk if the Japs sortie their fleet." Turner looked at Smith. "Can we agree to Makin?"

Smith nodded.

"Okay, you get a couple of your staff to work-up a preliminary draft with my people. I'll take their input and send a letter to Spruance and Nimitz for their approval to go to the Chiefs." Turner glanced at Captain Theiss and the Captain nodded his assent.

"I'd like to see it before it goes to Spruance," Smith said.

"Your staff will participate, but I'll send you a copy." Turner snarled.

"I'll send a supporting letter." Smith kept eye contact with Turner.

"Is there anything else we can do here today?" Turner asked, choosing to ignore Smith's comment.

"Kelly, I'd like to talk to you about the Betio landing." Smith looked around the room and swept his hand in an inclusive manner. "We don't need all these people here to cover what I want to talk about. They can go start putting together the information for the letter to the JCS."

Terrible Turner's face looked like a thunder cloud had passed over it. He knew what Smith wanted to discuss and had no desire to verbally wrestle with the General who looked more like an accountant than the hell-and-brimstone military leader he was. Turner's eyes narrowed. He knew Smith wouldn't take "no" for an answer. Howlin' Mad's genetic blood lines traced directly back to Patrick Henry and those genes were in evidence constantly. "We'll keep Erskine and Theiss here, the rest can go." Turner looked at his staff and motioned for them to leave with a head movement.

"Where do you want us to start?" Hogaboom asked.

Smith snapped, "Use your own judgment, Colonel Erskine will be there to assist you in a little while." Holland's staff quickly followed Turner's from the room. These men exchanged knowing glances, happy they wouldn't be involved in the argument that they felt sure would ensue, but curious as to the exact subject.

When the door closed, Turner stared at Smith. "I don't have a great deal of time, Holland. I hope this isn't in regard to the *timing* of the landing on Betio. We've been through that. The JCS is pushing me to schedule the Marshals operation in early January. I might get Nimitz to get us 30-days relief on that, but no more. We can't move GALVANIC back. It would have to go damn near to Christmas. They won't allow that."

"The Joint Chiefs won't have to wade through 500 yards of machine gun fire if the Higgins boats don't have enough water over those reefs to make it to the beaches. My men will. I don't want that on my conscience if there is any possibility to prevent it. There are two ways around that kind of slaughter. One is to change the date. The other is to expedite the shipment of the 50 LVTs of the newer model in transit somewhere. We don't know what the condition of the 125 being transferred up from the South Pacific is, so we need everyone. Those Alligators can climb right over the reefs and get my boys all the way to the seawall and inland. I want those LVTs for them."

"Damn it, Holland, we've been through this before, too. You're worrying about something that shouldn't be a problem. The estimated tides at "H" hour show the boats should have more than a foot of water clearance over the reef. Besides, the support fleet's bombardment of that little strip of sand will be so heavy nothing is going to be alive when your men go ashore."

"Yes, we've had this conversation before and we're going to keep having it until I'm comfortable I'm doing everything I can to save as many of my Marines as possible. What if the tide information is wrong? What if you don't wipe out most of the defenses on the beaches? That ship captain from New Zealand is positive we won't have enough tide to get across the reef in the Higgins boats. He lived on Betio. He's positive that during the days we have scheduled for the assault, there will be what he calls a dodging tide; the water just doesn't rise like normal. If that happens, we'll be dumping a couple thousand men out onto reefs. Everyone not in an Alligator will wade to the shore in knee to chest deep water. The distance is anywhere from 400 to 800 yards. Those men will face machine gun, mortar, sniper, and artillery fire. They'll be sitting ducks. Even if your bombardment is effective, I could lose 300 to 400 men killed and that many more wounded if they have to wade in." Smith's face was contorted into an angry mask.

"You're taking that one man's word and ignoring the

other members of the group advising us what tidal conditions should be." Turner swiveled his head to Theiss. "What are the staff boys calling them?"

"The Foreign Legion," Captain Theiss replied.

"Kelly, half the men in that group admit they don't know what the tides will really be like. The old skipper of the steamer *Niminoa* said he thought we'd be okay, but that the New Zealander's figures could very well be right. He said that the time of year was right for those dodging tides to occur. I don't want to gamble."

"You have enough of the LVT-1s to get your first wave and some of your second ashore. That will protect the men that normally take the worst beating. They can clean up any Japs that survive the pounding we're going to administer to them. Holland, you've got battleships, cruisers and destroyers hitting the targets on the little chunk of sand for hours before you land. Dive bombers will be working over anything that's left from the naval guns' bombardment and fighters strafing the beach right before your men come in." Turner was confident he was correct. "Sure, some will survive, but my bet is they'll be dazed and confused and won't put up much of a fight. No island defense has ever been subjected to the kind of shelling they'll experience. With the amount of ordnance we're dumping on that island, I'm not sure there'll be a whole lot left of it."

Smith tapped his fingers on the table in front of him.

"Kelly, I've seen artillery barrages in France during the last war that you'd swear a mouse couldn't live through if it were anywhere on that battlefield. Those artillery shells killed some of the enemy, but not all. Not even most of them. Every time we attacked across the fields their machine guns would open up and cause unimaginable casualties. I have respect for what you're going to try to do and hope you're as successful as you think you will be, but believe me, there is going to be plenty of fighting for us to do ashore. There are 4800 Japs waiting for us on that island. They'll be dug in and we'll have to burn and blast them out. I'll need every man I can get to the beach alive and full of fight."

"Do you know how that 4800 figure was estimated? That sounds like an awfully large garrison to defend such a small piece of sand." Turner wasn't happy discussing the issue further.

"Intelligence counted the number of latrines built on the piers over the water. We know what the Japanese field manuals call for—so many men per latrine. We just multiplied it out." Smith took a deep breath. "About the—"

Turner put both hands on the table, thrust his jaw out, and leaned over the top of the table toward Smith, interrupting him. "Holland, there isn't going to be any delay in the date. We're going on the 20th of November."

"Then get me those other LVTs for my men. They're

probably on the docks in the states." Smith was getting madder by the second.

"Part of them are and part of them aren't. You're not going to get them in time." Turner's expression and voice denoted finality.

Smith rose from the table and looked at Turner with cold intent eyes. Colonel Erskine followed his commander and stood up, too. Howlin' Mad said coldly, "No tractors, no invasion." He walked out of the conference room door followed closely by his chief of staff.

Captain Theiss looked at Terrible Turner, waiting for instruction.

Turner burned and cursed under his breath. Finally he said to the Captain, "Find those damned tractors and find some way to get them here on time."

23

"I Have Seen Hell and it is this Island"
1943, Ben Bennett
Island of Betio, Tarawa atoll

They wouldn't tell you, but they were—*scared.* Ben knew he was, even though it wasn't the disabling, paralyzing variety that some of his tractor mates were or would experience. Many of the young Marines around him were green replacements for men lost at Guadalcanal. Bennett hadn't been in the bitterest of the fighting during the early stages of that battle, but he'd fought there. He'd had bullets zip over his head, experienced the helpless panic that artillery shells bursting around you induces, he'd pulled the trigger of his Garand M-1 rifle in anger, seen and smelled death, endured the filth and privations an infantryman lives with—and he'd lost friends. Ben participated in the last desperate battles Japan waged for control of that island. He believed he knew what was coming. All the veterans around him had the same look Ben had on his face. He wondered what you'd call such an expression. Ben Bennett thought for a few seconds then decided it should be titled, *resigned apprehension.* He wondered why he would even be concerned about labeling such a thing. Ben was unaware that he'd become an *"old"* young man in the last year. He was just as oblivious of how much more war's corrosive nature would impact him in the next seventy-six hours.

Most of the replacements were ashen faced from a combination of gut wrenching fear and the bouncing and rolling of the LVT as it made its cork-like sojourn to the island. Some Marines deposited their recently eaten steak and eggs on the tractor's deck. Others kept their breakfast, but only with great difficulty. The first timers vainly tried to hide the terror that gripped their souls and clawed at their hearts. The nervousness in their flitting glances betrayed them. One or two still sported an adolescent image of what they were about to be thrown into; they appeared eager for battle. Ben wondered how they'd feel the first time they saw a fellow Marine disintegrate in the center of a shell burst or when a friend was stitched with machine gun fire. Maybe the pre-landing talks delivered by the officers leading the assault had convinced them that the fighting would not be as terrible as he presumed it would be.

Ben remembered the words of his Commanding Officer describing the naval bombardment, the heaviest ever to try to obliterate the enemy on a hostile beach. It would be rough, but fast, Ben had been told. He had tried to maintain a sense of optimism as he scurried down the cargo net. Ben wanted to believe there would barely be enough sand left to walk on when the battleships, cruisers, destroyers and aircraft finished pummeling the island. When the clocks reached 0606 and the first big naval shells sped for the island, the Marines cheered. Watching the flame and smoke erupt from the horizon, Ben hoped his Commanding Officer's words might be true. He knew that his CO, Major Schoettel, was telling his men what he believed was the honest "word."

Ben was typical of the men around him. He had faith in his officers. He had faith in his country. He had faith in the Marine Corps. But, Ben also was a realist. The fire fights he'd been in seldom went precisely as planned. More often, they only bore a slight resemblance to what the troops were told to expect. The enemy always had other ideas.

In the tractors containing the Marines' first assault wave was Ben's reinforced rifle platoon of company "J," 3rd Battalion, 2nd Marine regiment. As Bennett's LVT crossed the line of departure, Ben knew that being assigned to the first wave increased his chances of being killed or wounded. He and his buddies would be the first to hit their assigned beach and be exposed to murderous fire from surviving Japanese in their pillboxes and emplacements. It was a sobering thought.

* * *

Far ahead lay the low outline of the island almost obscured by the pale of smoke, dust and bright explosions coating it. As the tractor covered the remaining 2000 yards to the sand, he waited for the inevitable shelling and bullets to seek out his tractor. Watching the island, he noted that some shells fired by the Navy's big guns were passing over the island and striking the water beyond. He hoped that the fleet wasn't missing with a large part of their bombardment. Each shell that failed to hit the island meant there was a better chance for the survival of Japanese soldiers and less chance for Ben and his buddies.

Aircraft from the carriers accompanying the invasion force had completed their dive bombing and strafing attacks during a planned break in the naval bombardment. The ships big guns had resumed their cannonade. The island was taking a fearful beating. As they relentlessly closed the distance, Ben could see that most of the tops of the palm tress were blown off and rubble remained of what had been buildings. His hopes rose until one of the veterans next to him yelled, "Incoming!" All the Marines ducked. A sharp whistle was followed by an explosion a hundred feet behind them. It had started.

* * *

The first bullets reached the LVT just before its tracks crunched into the coral of the island's fringing reef. The occasional strike soon sounded like hail hitting a roof. The tractor lurched upward on the coral, exposing most of the tractor before it tilted downward into the slightly deeper water inside the reefs edge. He heard someone go "uumph," followed immediately by someone yelling, "Sam's hit." A couple of larger caliber bullets penetrated right through the armor plating that tried to protect the Marines inside. Ben peeked at the island as the tractor ground along the coral bottom in waist deep water. The beach was still 300 to 400 yards away. He could make out the naked trunks of defoliated palm trees, the low line that was the seawall he'd been briefed to expect. Machine gun fire from the seawall and immediately behind it made mini water geysers that swept around his LVT and the tractors to his right. He quickly ducked below the tractor's side for cover from the death zipping over his head.

The drivers yelled at the man firing the .30 caliber machine gun at their enemy, "Damn, Jimmy, those boats ain't gonna clear that reef. Not at all. We didn't have more'n a foot a water where we went over."

Jimmy wasn't concerned with the problems the Higgins boats would have getting across the reef. Machine gun bullets beat against the tractor's front and sides—Jimmy saw where they were coming from. He screamed, "For Christ's sake go to the left, you're driving us into a strong point." The driver angled the LVT slightly to the left. "More, damn it, more!" the gunner insisted.

As the last words cleared his mouth, the whoosh of a mortar shell threw salt water inside the LVT and peppered the sides with shrapnel. The driver turned the tractor even more sharply to the left. The stream of machine gun bullets became intermittent, not steady. Jimmy yelled to the driver, "Not any more, we're gonna miss Red-1 and end up landing on Red-2."

The driver corrected his course slightly to the right. He asked the gunner, "Jimmy, how's that?" The gunner didn't answer. Ben looked up as the driver cursed. Jimmy was slumped against the back of his 30 caliber Browning air cooled machine gun. His head was turned to the side and rested on the thumb triggers of the gun. A bloody hole had replaced his right eye. Ben heard the man next to him gasp as he slipped to the floor. Ben bent over to try to help the man, a replacement he was just getting to know. The Marine stared up at him with unseeing eyes. Blood gushed from a large hole at the base of his throat and from his mouth then stopped abruptly. Ben remembered that the fellow's name was Mark and that he liked playing the trumpet. He'd never have the opportunity again.

Ben heard the driver say, "Shit!" A trickle of blood ran down his forearm onto one of the control levers. Sergeant Ezra Stark pushed his way back to the driver. Ben heard the sergeant ask, "Are you okay, can you still drive?"

"It just nicked my arm," the driver answered. "I'm good. Hey, can you man that 30 cal? Maybe you can suppress some of that fire coming out at us."

"Yeah," Stark growled. He wasn't enthusiastic about the prospects for what he was about to do. He told everybody as he went from the rear to the front of the LVT, "Keep those heads down and be ready to move." He eased the dead gunner out of the way and fired the machine gun toward the seawall ahead of the tractor.

The tractor reeled and swayed as it passed over some uneven bottom before leveling out again making its way to the beach. There was a loud explosion to the side of the LVT. Ben saw another tractor had been hit by an artillery shell and was burning profusely. He saw a couple men roll over the side before bullets zipped over his tractor forcing him to duck. The driver yelled, "The Japs have guns set up on that pier to our left." Ben looked at the driver. The man was crouched as low as he could get trying to present as small a target as possible. Stark called back, "Watch that tetrahedron!" The driver made a violent maneuver to avoid the obstacle. Stark was talking again, "Make sure you get us through that barbwire." The driver grunted his assent and after a glance at the shore he said, "We're going into Red-2." The crescendo of fire from the Japanese positions became ever greater, the noise making it difficult to hear.

Ben took a quick peek out the front. They were getting

close to the seawall; only seconds remained before he'd be leaping over the side into the hail of bullets flying all around them. A roar sounded as a shell of some variety exploded a few yards to the right of the LVT. "Be ready," Stark screamed. The tractor thudded to a halt and the tracks tore at the coconut logs that made the seawall. The tractor lifted into the air in front as it tried to scale the wall but tumbled back with a thump. Stark yelled, "This is it. Everybody out!"

Two of his friends, Weber and Schmidt, were already rolling over the side trying to keep as low of a profile as possible. He heard Weber yell his nickname,"3B go to the other side." Ben quickly moved across the LVT and prepared to go over the top. Corporal Contorno vaulted out of the tractor. The driver was screaming, "Get out! Get out! Get out! I've got to get this thing off the beach!" Just as Bennett was prepared to jump, the man next to him lifted up to get out. A burst of machine gun fire that sounded like it was right in front of the tractor ripped the man into shreds sending him back into the LVT and onto Ben. They both fell on the vehicle's deck. Ben scrambled up. He felt the Tractor back up and begin to turn. Bennett didn't think; he grasped his rifle and flung himself over the side, fully expecting to feel burning bullets tearing into his body. In what seemed like minutes, but was only a second, his body fell to the sand below. He landed on his elbows and knees.

Ben half walked and half crawled the twenty-five feet to the seawall's base.

He checked his rifle and looked around for the other members of his squad. A blur behind Ben caused him to turn and stare at the scene unfolding on the reef and beyond. The LVT he had just ridden in on was moving as rapidly as it could back toward the lagoon. In the driver's haste, he drove over a dead Marine lying in the shallow water. More tractors were nearing the shore. Several LVTs were victims of artillery or mortar shells. They burned bright orange and threw oily black smoke into the air. Men struggled through the lagoon waters from disabled tractors. Bodies already dotted the sea.

"Weber, 3B, Schmidt, over here." Corporal Contorno yelled. Ben saw the man crouched behind the sea wall ten yards away. Making sure he stayed bent over low enough that his body was lower than the seawall's top, he trotted over to Contorno. Weber and Schmidt were close behind. Ben passed several other Marines who huddled against the seawall. Some he recognized, some he didn't.

The Corporal pointed to a hole in the top of the seawall. Just before he spoke a stream of bullets fired from a Nambu heavy machine gun screamed out at the Marines in LVTs and those struggling in the water. Contorno said, "We're going after that gun. Weber and 3B, you stay here and cover us with your rifles. One of you, keep your eyes on the area right above the opening. If they know we're out here one of the Nips will try to shoot us from the top. Schmidt, you come with me. You're my back up. If I don't get a grenade in the hole with that gun, you have to do it. We'll use our rifles to be sure they're dead after the grenade explodes."

Contorno and Schmidt crawled along the wall to a spot a yard away from the embrasure. Weber said, "I'll keep watch on the wall above the emplacement. You scan around."

Bennett said, "Okay."

Contorno removed a grenade from his belt and motioned for Schmidt to do the same. They both pulled the pins and on Contorno's signal both tossed the grenades into the opening. Schmidt and Contorno flattened themselves on the ground. Within two seconds the grenades exploded inside the gun emplacement with a pair of muffled roars. Contorno immediately got to his feet, shoved his rifle through the hole, and peered inside. He fired six times and started to come back along the seawall followed by Schmidt.

Ben took his eyes off the top of the seawall and glanced at his watch. It read 9:12. Shell fire exploding behind him drew his attention to the lagoon. The second wave of LVTs was approaching the beach. It was obvious the Japanese strategy was to shift its fire from those who reached the beach to those who were on their way to the shore. Disabled and burning LVTs dotted the waters. Bennett watched as men who abandoned their LVTs were shot and dropped in the water spreading red stains in the blue lagoon. It was sickening . . . and enraging. Ben wanted to kill the enemy slaughtering his brother Marines.

"Contorno, get those men and get over here." Sergeant Stark waved his arm motioning for the Corporal, Weber, Bennett, and the rest to join him.

As Ben turned to follow Contorno, he glanced at the top of the seawall. The tip of a bayonet appeared over the top palm log followed by an Arisika rifle muzzle. Ben raised his rifle aiming it at the area above the Japanese weapon. The Japanese mushroom-shaped helmet popped up over the wall followed by the man's head and shoulders. Ben fired twice and screamed a warning, "Look out!" Ben's bullets struck the Jap soldier and he pitched forward onto the seawall laying draped over it.

Two more Japanese appeared above. Before Ben could swing his rifle to shoot, the Marines around him poured rifle bullets into the two soldiers. Both dropped like rag dolls, behind the seawall, out of Ben's vision.

Stark yelled at them frantically, "Hold your position, don't move." During the brief encounter Ben and his buddies had with the three Japanese Imperial Marines, the Sergeant attempted to cross the seawall with five men only to find they were right in front of another machine gun position. Two of his men were killed instantly and lay at the base of the seawall. Stark took a bullet in the fleshy part of his upper arm. The other two Marines made it over the seawall and found cover in a shell hole a few feet on the island side. At that instant, one hundred yards away, a gigantic explosion at a point inland from where the huge pier joined the shore shook the ground and momentarily stunned everyone. Debris rained down on startled Americans and Japanese. Contorno said, "Ammunition dump of some kind." Ben found out later it was the main torpedo storage area for the Japanese airfield.

Ben pressed against the seawall and looked out to the lagoon. The second wave of tractors was just reaching the beach. One Marine-filled tractor, fifty yards to his right, found a low spot on the seawall, ground up and over it to the cheers of the Marines huddled in the defilade the wall provided. Other LVTs weren't all faring as well. Several were burning or disabled. A few had broken down. Marines that had been forced into the water tried to get to shore, some moving as fast as they could to gain the beach and cover, others stayed as low in the water as they could to present as small a target as possible. Neither strategy worked well. The Japanese gunners mercilessly sprayed the wading Marines, creating dark humps in the water surrounded with red rings from the dying men's blood. It infuriated Ben. The fact that he was helpless to stop the massacre frustrated him immensely.

For the first time, Ben realized he had accepted the fact he'd probably die, possibly in minutes. He gritted his teeth and swore a solemn silent oath repeated innumerable times on those tortured sands by men of both sides, *I may die, but I'm going to kill some of my enemies before I do.*

His attention returned to the tragedy unfolding behind him. The Higgins boats containing reinforcements in the latter waves had reached the reef and found they could not pass over it. Some dropped their ramps on the reef forcing the Marines disgorging from the boat to struggle through as much as 800 yards of water and deadly enemy fire. Others stopped short unwittingly sending heavily laden men rushing into ten to fifteen feet of water. The lucky ones were able to release their loads and swim or scramble along the bottom to the reef. Many drowned. Still other boats, seeing the slaughter and mayhem, circled at the reef's edge looking for an alternative.

Ben realized he was witnessing the deaths of hundreds of fellow Marines. The water at the fringe and inside the reef turned pink from Marine blood. He cursed under his breath. Ben remembered his apprehension and how he felt he'd had bad luck to be in the first wave. Now, watching the fate of the men in the boats, he was thankful he had been. As he stared at the grizzly giant horror movie, the first tractors returning from the beach realized the plight of the wading troops and the Marines being left at the outer edge of the reef. The tractor drivers began to pick up Marines and made brave return trips to the beach. Other tractors sought wounded, hauled them aboard and headed for the transports and medical help.

A series of explosions and a whooshing sound from somewhere over the seawall returned his thoughts to his own survival. He knew the sound—it was a flame thrower. Ben sincerely hoped it was a Marine weapon, not Japanese. He'd seen the results these harbingers from hell had on their victims and if there was *one way* he *didn't* want to die it was *that way.*

Sergeant Starks yelled, "Okay guys, lets get off this beach. Find cover as quick as you can once you're across the wall." He hesitated then said, "Go . . . NOW!" He rose and half the men in J Company stood and struggled up and over the seawall into the unknown terrors that lay beyond. Of those that remained, half were too frightened to respond; half would never rise again.

"Let's go 3B," Weber said. Ben was already half way over the wall. He snuck a peek at the three Japs he and his comrades shot just moments before, but which seemed like months ago. They lay in the sand like broken manikins. Thirty feet ahead, Bennett saw a slit trench and jumped down into it, ready for hand to hand combat if his enemy was there. His Japanese trench-mates were dead, probably the victims of Navy fighters that strafed the beach. Weber dropped into the trench followed by Contorno.

"Where's Schmidt?" Weber asked.

Corporal Contorno shook his head, his eyes saying all that was needed.

Huddled in the trench, Ben glanced at his watch—10:12—just one hour. It seemed like a lifetime had past. Soberly, Ben realized—for Schmidt, it had.

* * *

A cloud of gray dust hung above him. Mixed with it was the stench of 4800 Japanese and 1000 Marine dead. Ben looked at his watch again. The hands pointed to 4:12 PM. That was seventy-nine hours after the first time he'd looked at it. It seemed more like seventy-nine years to Bennett. He was awaiting a ride to the hospital aboard ship to do more permanent repairs to his damaged body. Sitting behind the beach and close to the pier, Ben was near the point where he'd jumped from the LVT those three plus days before. A Navy corpsman bandaged his wounds when he returned to the beach, now a beehive of activity. The Seabees already were getting their equipment ready to put the airstrip he'd fought over and around for two days back in service.

Two of his wounds were superficial. One bullet had grazed his left shoulder. Spent shrapnel from a mortar shell sliced his dungaree pants and put a shallow three inch slice in his thigh. The third wound was more significant. Just a few hours before the island was secured, a Jap soldier had charged the foxhole Ben was in and shot down into it as Ben was aiming his rifle at his attacker. They shot simultaneously. The Japanese bullet hit Bennett in the left wrist, passing through it and chipping one of the bones, exited, then reentered his upper arm coming to rest somewhere inside. Like many of his fellow Marines, Ben fought until his unit was taken out of the line and returned to the beach.

Sergeant Stark sat next to him. Both men were perched on their helmets. The two Marines' four days' beard growth was covered with dust and grime and they smelled of stale sweat. Their eyes were fixed in the vacant stare peculiar to men who have just experienced battle. Each was silent, buried in his own thoughts. A third of Stark's face was covered with a bandage protecting the wound caused by a bullet that went through his jaw, his major wound. Another swath of blood-soaked white encased one calf below the knee. The third his upper arm, suffered in the first minutes of the landing.

"Hey, you two." The Navy Corpsman called to them from a few feet away. "You guys' turn. You go back in a LCVP. The number is 274. They'll be somebody down there to help you. It's down next to the pier. On the East side."

Ben rose and helped Stark to his feet. "Ready, Sergeant?"

Stark nodded, speech was painful. They limped and shuffled toward the pier, so tired each step was an effort. With each tortured stride they took, both gained a measure of relief for the realization they had survived grew stronger. So was their sadness. Their friends Schmidt, Contorno and many others would never leave.

As Ben boarded the LCVP, a sailor dressed in clean fatigues said, "It was really bad, wasn't it?"

Ben answered, "I have seen Hell and it is this island."

24

An Old Scar, a Renewed Man
2009, Ben Bennett
Kiribati, the Island of Betio, Tarawa atoll

"Grandpa, where did you come ashore? You said something about a pier?" Bennett's grandson had rejoined him, the questions he asked brought Ben back from his travel to the past.

Ben looked down the beach. He closed his eyes trying to visualize the terrain as it was in 1943. His mind pictured the western tip of the island and the cove. That was Red 1. He ignored the corpses strewn on the beach and floating in the lagoon accompanying that image. His mind's vision moved closer to him, past the remembered rubble of the Japanese strong-point built where landing beach Red 1 and Red 2 joined. He opened his eyes relating his memories to what now lay in front of him. His mind traversed the straight seawall section of beach Red 2 as it crept toward the pier. Without the landmarks he remembered—the airstrip, the pier, the log seawall—it was difficult to be exact, but when he closed his eyes . . . . Ben opened his eyes and pointed. The wooden pier he remembered had been replaced by an earthen fill changing the very contour of the beach. "It was right about there."

"Do you want to go down there, Dad?' Andrew Bennett asked as he walked up to rejoin his father.

Ben Bennett stared at the bit of beach that came so close to killing him. Emotions tugged at him both ways. He wanted to, but it was something that might challenge him for the control of his emotions, a control in which he took pride. He remained silent.

"Grandpa, would you like to go there alone?" Ben's grandson asked. He knew his grandfather to be a private person; one who guarded his inner self. "We'll all go back down with the kids."

"I think I'd like that." Ben looked at that small point of land to keep from making eye contact. "There are some things that are too personal to share; I hope you all understand that."

"Dad, can you make it down there okay?" Andrew looked concerned. His father wouldn't even admit to himself that he couldn't and shouldn't still be capable of doing what he had done when aged forty. Knee and hip replacement only seemed to make him more determined to take physical chances that weren't always wise. Andrew expected his father to bristle at the suggestion.

Ben looked at his son. "Yes, I'll be fine and I'll be careful. But, Andrew, if you *want* to go *part way* with me, it's alright."

Andrew scanned his father's face, then said, "No, Dad, I think you should go alone if you don't think you'll have any problems."

Ben's son turned and said, "Let's go back to check out the kids." He started toward the youngsters playing at the water's edge. Slowly, all of Ben Bennett's family walked the beach, each turning their heads toward him frequently in a sign of silent support.

Ben watched them for several seconds before he turned his focus on the spot of sand he'd identified earlier. When he took his first step, he felt a strange transition taking place. Each stride he took blurred the color and details of today's surroundings. The hands on time's clock were spinning backwards. He stopped for an instant as he approached the location that had been the pier head—at the place he'd waited to be evacuated. Yes, the pier had returned, its wooden structure ending close to where the Japanese torpedo dump exploded. The earthen fill was gone, the old structure looked the same. He thought of Stark and Weber, of Schmidt and Contorno. He sighed and plodded on. Ben passed the pier head and the place where he'd sat on his helmet, where he wondered if he was really leaving the Hell he'd been in or if he was dead and his spirit was being led away. As he neared the spot, *his spot*, the palm trees lost all their foliage, the sand was again strewn with bits of buildings and other flotsam of war. In his mind, the past had returned. One foot followed the other until he felt more than saw he was at the right spot. He knew *it was here.*

Ben saw things the way they had been. He gasped and felt weak. This wasn't what he expected. Ben sat down on something; he wasn't sure what. At his feet, were the logs of the old seawall; beneath it was the beach. In the lagoon, the dead had returned, bobbing like corks in the tepid waters. Red rings appeared around each man as if to highlight him. His head turned slightly to his left. The lone Japanese soldier he'd shot lay there, but not as Ben had last saw him. The soldier lay face up, staring that unseeing gaze Ben had observed too often. As Ben watched, the face began to deteriorate. It quickly changed color, rotting in greens, blues, and blacks. Maggots came and soon the skull was exposed. Ben flinched leaning away from the corpse.

"Steady, 3B." A voice close to him said calmly. Ben looked around wildly. A Marine stood next to and slightly behind him. Dressed in dirty dungaree fatigues with his helmet on his head, the young man had a familiar look, a familiar voice, a familiar smell, a familiar posture. Ben strained his eyes trying to see the man's features, but past a scruffy beard, they wouldn't come into focus. The man was outfitted for combat. His canvas belt had several ammunition pouches snapped to it, two canteens hung around the man's waist and a Kabar combat knife extended from the belt down his side. Camouflage netting covered his helmet. A grenade was attached to the man's back pack straps that cut into his shoulders. Dusty boondockers completed the familiar image.

"It's not easy to come back," the voice continued. "You want to come, but after you get here, it's hard, isn't it?"

Ben stared at the Marine standing next to him. "Yes, it is," Ben answered. The Marine looked out at the lagoon with his arms folded across his chest.

"What do you think, 3B? Was what happened here worth it?" The young man in the dungarees continued to stare out into the lagoon.

Ben looked at the spot where the Japanese soldier was seconds before. The body was gone, only the palm log wall remained. Ben blinked his eyes, but said nothing.

"Do you think this was a mistake? Do you regret being here?" The Marine asked.

"That's not easy to answer. I never believed it was a mistake. I've always been proud of what we did here. But . . . standing on this spot . . . remembering . . . ." Ben looked out on the blue water with its cargo of dead men and pink dyed measles.

"Isn't answering that question part of the reason you came here?'

Ben thought for several seconds. "Yes, I guess it is."

"So, do you think the U.S. had to go to war with Japan

and Germany?" The Marine was prompting Ben's mental process.

"Yes. The only alternative was to let the Japs and Nazis do what they wanted. Roosevelt tried using embargoes, sanctions and negotiations. Hell, the Japanese had a delegation in Washington to discuss maintaining peace the day they bombed Pearl Harbor. We saw what the Japanese did in China and had some idea what was happening in Europe. We didn't have a choice." Ben sounded confident about his thoughts. "I've never doubted fighting Japan was the correct decision for the U.S. to make. Or Germany."

"Then what are you having doubts about; is it what happened here?"

Ben dropped his gaze to the seawall. "It was part of the war. Tarawa and this island was the first amphibious attack against a heavily defended island. After the war, Holland Smith said Betio was a mistake. I don't think it was one that could have been avoided. There's always a first time and an unknown. If it wasn't here, it would have been somewhere else—maybe Nauru or Truk. Until we took Betio, no one really knew what to expect. Everybody learned from it. No, I don't think this was a mistake and I don't regret being here. Hindsight is 20-20. It was just the fate of the 2nd Marines to draw this assignment and my fate to be part of the 2nd Marines."

"But, that doesn't answer your whole question does it?"

The Marine swept one hand toward the lagoon. "You feel we paid too big of a cost?"

"Maybe at this battle, I'm not sure about that. But the war, itself? No. The price of losing would have been far greater." Ben thought for a moment. "My disappointment is that it appears we're going to go through this again—but I fear our country may not be up to the challenge this time."

"Why's that?"

"We don't have leaders like we did. The politicians in Washington are too busy fighting over who controls what, making their special interest friends rich and making the other party look bad. They can't even see that the countries laws are enforced. You see it every day. And, as a people, we've grown soft. We've become a country of fat, complacent sheep that are more interested in political correctness than honest competition to become a winner."

The Marine dropped his head. He sounded sad as he said, "If that's true, we failed here."

Ben and the man next to him looked out at the lagoon. They shared a silent moment. The marine shook his head slowly, "All those lives—wasted. If that's what's happened . . . Well, I agree with you, except who is responsible."

Bennett scanned the blurred face of the Marine and asked, "What do you mean? Who do you think is responsible?"

"You are," the dungaree clad man said.

"Why?" was Ben's shocked reply.

"Because, 3B, you watched it happen and haven't stopped it."

"What can I do? I'm just another citizen. You have to be a politician, some big-time TV or movie person, or a big-wig in a political party to affect what's happening." An indignant Ben felt he was legitimately defending himself from an accusation he'd never expected to be leveled at him.

"I'm sure you vote, but do you really explore the positions of the person running for office or vote by the party the individual is representing?'

Ben looked less offended. "There are a lot of people running for office."

"There were a lot of people running for office in 1940, too. What made that so different?"

Bennett hung his head and looked back out to sea. "One person just can't make a difference."

"You know that isn't true. What about Donald Roebling and Andrew Higgins. They weren't elected officials. They made a difference. You know that's true. How many congressional offices have you visited? How many senators have you written? How many local political offices have you tried to hold? How many anti-kook protests against left or right-wing extremists have you organized or participated in? How many newspapers, TV, or radio shows have you taken time to contact to express your opinion of what they're disseminating? You don't know what your personal power is until you exercise it. You'll find you have much more strength than you think, but you'll never know until you try."

"I'm afraid I'm too old. I still have the energy, but who'd listen to me?"

"Remember Holland Smith? There were people that said he was too old. He fought and won. He made people listen to him! If you really feel strongly about what you see as problems preserving what we fought for here, isn't it worth trying to correct what's wrong at any age? You don't have to run a hundred yard dash to pick up a pen."

Ben looked at the Marine dressed in his dirty rumpled uniform. Ben's vision slowly elevated to his face. "Yes, you're right. I've got to try and keep trying." Ben spoke with conviction and as he did the man's face came into clear focus. He had been speaking to the young 3B. Ben was speaking to himself.

"You okay, old fellow?" Ben felt a hand on his shoulder, today returned. The lagoon was unscarred blue, no bodies marred its beauty, no red dyed its waters. The log seawall was replaced by a concrete retainer. The hand belonged to a young Polynesian man whose concern was etched in his features. He'd evidently overheard Ben's mumblings. Bennett found *he was sitting on a bench at the shores edge, at the point he'd landed 43 years before.*

"Yes, I'm fine." Ben stood and stretched. "I hope you didn't mind me sitting on your bench."

"Oh, it's not mine." The man paused and said very sincerely. "I just wanted to be sure you were alright." The brown face asked. "Were you reliving something from your past?"

"I think you know I was. And yes, I was here then."

"My people say, what has come before, has left, so leave it. It is like the mirage of an island on the ocean; it is one you can never reach. Were you reaching for something in your past?"

Ben looked at the man and smiled, "No, something from my future."

There was liveliness in Ben Bennett's step as he strode toward his family. It was the rejuvenated strength that conviction and purpose always brings.

Afterword

A word about the fate of the historical characters that provided the skeleton over which I stretched the story fabric of *Blue Water, Red Blood* is in order. They are exceptional men; men that our leaders of today could profit from by observing their example.

Andrew Jackson Higgins was born August 28, 1886, in Columbus, Nebraska. Higgins had been in the lumber business in the employ of various companies before starting his own enterprise in New Orleans during 1922. Because a large part of his commerce was import and export, Andrew purchased a fleet of ships. To build, maintain and modify his boats, he opened a shipyard. One of the problems he faced was moving logs from and supplies to locations without established docks. Often these logging camps were in areas along the Gulf of Mexico's coast line and the rivers flowing into it. These camps' landing sites were shallow and hard to access. He originally developed the Eureka motorized barge to service these locations. It was designed to operate in very shallow water, be highly maneuverable, and to load and unload without the assistance of a pier.

Eventually, Higgins withdrew from the lumber business but remained in shipbuilding. Through dealings with the

Coast Guard, he learned of a possible application for the Eureka to solve the Navy's problem of providing a Landing Craft for its Marine Corp branch. After the struggle with naval bureaucrats and through the dogged support of the Marines, Higgin's boats became one of the most important elements in US amphibious warfare both in the Pacific and Europe. His factories produced over 20,000 craft including, LCVPs, LCIs, LCMs and PT boats. Collectively, these boats became known as "Higgins Boats." He also made torpedo tubes, gun turrets and other defense components. Used at Normandy on D-Day, Higgins boats are seen in the opening scenes of the epic Speilberg-Hanks movie, "Saving Private Ryan."

Higgins' highly successful business closed shortly after the close of the war, Andrew going into semi-retirement. The contribution he and his equipment made to the war effort was widely recognized and he was given many citations and testimonials. Dwight Eisenhower said, "Andrew Higgins is the man who won the war for us. If he hadn't designed his boat, our whole war strategy would have had to been different."

Higgins passed away on August 1, 1952, at 66. He is buried in his beloved New Orleans at the Metairie Cemetery.

Holland McTyeire Smith was born on April 20, 1882, in Seale, Alabama. From a family that held strong confederate traditions, his parents refused to allow him to accept an appointment to West Point because of their animosity toward the government. He received a BS from Auburn and his Law degree from the University of Alabama. Smith found that he didn't like practicing law and he soon gravitated to the Marines. Here he found a life-long commitment to the Corps he loved.

Smith's career was one filled with controversy as illustrated in *Blue Water, Red Blood*. Unafraid to reproach superiors when he believed he was correct, his stubborn aggressiveness was the secret of his successes and failures. He spent his career trying to advance the capabilities and fortunes of the Corps which he championed so doggedly. Howlin' Mad may have been a hard task master in command, but he also had a steel hard core when it came to protecting the troops that fought for him. The irony is that he became the man responsible for some of the most costly battles fought by any US ground troops. He was called a "butcher," "cold-blooded murderer," and "indiscriminate waster of human life," for it fell to him to have to command the bloodiest part of the Pacific war; one from which there was no alternative as to where and how the battles were fought. As James Forrestal, Secretary of the Navy commented to a critic about that portion of the war, "There is no short or easy way." Smith didn't select the places the Marines fought, he carried out the orders.

After the portion of Smith's life covered in this novel, he commanded the Marines in their sweep across the Central Pacific that included invading the Gilbert, Marshall, Mariana island groups and ended with the landings on Iwo Jima. Howlin' Mad's combativeness and perfectionism created problems between him and the Army during the invasion of Saipan where he relieved an Army General (also named Smith), whom he felt was endangering his Marine troops on that island. While supported by his superiors in the Navy, the incident cast a cloud over his career that never fully cleared. Eventually, he was "promoted upstairs," out of combat. Holland retired from the Corps on May 15, 1946.

Holland Smith wrote a very interesting autobiography entitled *Coral and Brass* that is a good read and recounts his view of his career, his relations with the Navy/Army brass, and the Marines sweep across the Pacific. Smith passed away on January 12, 1967 at the US Naval Hospital in San Diego at 84. He is the Patton of the Pacific in my opinion.

Donald Roebling was born November 15, 1908, in New York City. The Roebling family was one of the most prominent in America in the early 1900s. Donald was the grandson of Washington A. Roebling who designed and built the Brooklyn Bridge. His son, and Don's father, John A. Roebling, was president of the Roebling Cable and Wire Rope Company, the family business. John Roebling emerged as one of the largest and most powerful financiers in the first quarter of the 20th century.

Early in Donald's childhood it became apparent that he would be a challenge for his parents and others who dealt with him. Though very intelligent, he didn't take his studies seriously and spent time in a boarding school that was supposed to be a remedy, but which proved fruitless. His addiction to sweets and the resulting extreme obesity further isolated him from his peers and impacted his behavior. Young Roebling was very generous to associates, endeavoring to curry favor and friendship. Donald decided against maintaining the family tradition of attending engineering college, instead opting to go to the Bliss Mathematics Institute. Within six months Bliss had asked Donald to leave the school because of the constant barrage of problems the teaching staff had with him. After returning from school, his eccentricities created many problems at his parents' residence. At twenty, Donald Roebling moved out of the family's New Jersey home and ended up living in Clearwater, Florida.

Concerned about his 400 pound son's welfare and direction in life, John Roebling helped establish young Donald in his own construction business. Though hoping Donald would find purpose and direction in his life, John didn't deny his son access to the family treasures. Challenging Donald to develop the amphibious Hurricane Res-

291

emerged as one of the largest and most powerful financiers in the first quarter of the 20th century.

cue Vehicle was his father's successful method of accomplishing that end. In fact, the development of the Alligator became Donald Roebling's purpose in life, and accompanied the conviction that he was put on earth to assist others.

Donald Roebling maintained that conviction and purpose for the rest of his life. The successful development of the Alligator and its transformation into the LVT tractors saved literally thousands of U.S. Marine lives in the Pacific battles in World War II. His adamant refusal to profit in any way from the development of the LVT, his dedicated efforts to accelerate engineering of the tractor to have it available to use in time for the Pacific offensive, and his selfless efforts to aid with the defense of his nation earned Roebling a Medal of Merit presented to him by President Harry S. Truman in 1948.

His philanthropy became legend in the West Central Florida area. Donald's footprints bearing evidence of his kindness and desire to do good remain there and in other areas around our country today.

Though he remarried a couple more times and became a community leader, he continued marching to the sound of drums not heard by others. Unable to curb his obsessions and suffering from the results of some of his eccentricities, Donald Roebling died at the young age of 50 on the 29th August, 1959, in Boston, Massachusetts.

About Author D.L. Havlin

D.L. Havlin is an eclectic author whose rich, varied background mirrors his novels, novellas, and short stories. Born April 18, 1941 he's packed three lifetimes of experiences into one brim full existence. He believes, "The one big advantage writing at an advanced age provides is that life is what you know and not what you project it might be."

Schooled in Ft Myers, Florida, Anderson H.S., in Cincinnati, Ohio, and the University of Cincinnati, his widely varied career included: systems analyst, procedure writer, production manager, materials manager, licensed boat captain, fishing guide, high school football coach, product sales manager, manufacturing manager, world-wide divisional customer service director, chemicals distributor general manager, call center tech service rep, newspaper reporter, president and general manager of a small manufacturing company.

An avid lover of the outdoors and sports enthusiast, his passion for fishing, hunting, and camping are frequently included in his writing. A deep love for nature and especially wild Florida often furnish settings for his work, but his travels make places such as Kiev, Singapore, London, New York, Modena, or Saxonhausen backgrounds for his stories as well.

His unique combination of vivid imagination and ability to weave intricate plot lines, seasoned by his life-time exposure to fascinating story possibilities, provides the heart-felt, enjoyable reading his novels

293

provide. DL is dedicated to the theory that readers are thinkers and one of his favorite responses to anyone questioning the assertion is "Open minds, open books.".

He answers, "Why do you write?" by saying, "To entertain—that's first, but to provoke thought is a close second. I firmly believe both are done through the heart, for the mind is seldom opened until it is emotionally conditioned to respond."

Made in the USA
Charleston, SC
09 October 2012